We hope you enjoy this book. Please return or renew it by the due date.

You can renew it at www.norfolk.gov.uk/libraries or by using our free library app.

Otherwise you can phone 0344 800 8020 - please have your library card and PIN ready.

You can sign up for email reminders too.

NORFOLK ITEM

30129 091 749 953

D1419231

PEARSON

Pearson Education Limited,
Edinburgh Gate, Harlow,
Essex CM20 2JE, England
and Associated Companies throughout the world.
www.pearson.co.za

First published by 1977
First published as Longman African Classic 1988
First published as Longman African Writers 1994
20 19 18 17 16 15
IMP 24 23 22 21 20 19

Set in Baskerville

ISBN 978-0-582-30845-9

Ama Ata Aidoo, one of Africa's leading feminist writers, was born and educated in Ghana. She obtained a B.A. degree in English at the University of Ghana and has taught at universities in Ghana, Tanzania and Kenya. Her concerns as a writer, a woman and a teacher of literature have encouraged her to travel and lecture extensively in Africa, Europe and North America.

Her first novel *Our Sister Killjoy*, a collection of short stories, *No Sweetness Here* and her plays *The Dilemma of a Ghost* and *Anowa* are all published in the LONGMAN AFRICAN WRITERS series.

Ama Ata Aidoo continues to write short stories, radio plays and poetry.

Contents

For You
Nanabanyin Tandoh,
who knows how to build;
people
structures
lives . . .

and

Roger Genoud
the son of Marcel Genoud:

The news came on a
hot stormy noon –
and
there was no cloth
strong enough to
hold my spilling intestines in.
The Sun, confused,
ran away to hide
unable to explain
why
This Worker
should be laid off so soon.

His heart and his mind
both raced double time –
so
he could still feel
knowing what he knew.

That Valiant One
was from Bernex.

Into a Bad Dream

Things are working out

towards their dazzling conclusions . . .

. . . so it is neither here nor there,
what ticky-tackies we have
saddled and surrounded ourselves with,
blocked our views,
cluttered our brains.

What is frustrating, though, in arguing with a nigger who is a 'moderate' is that since the interests he is so busy defending are not even his own, he can regurgitate only what he has learnt from his bosses for you. Like:

The need for law and order;

The gravest problem facing mankind being hunger, disease, and ignorance;

On hijackings as a deliberate attempt to hold decent society to ransom;

The sanctity of the U.N. charter;

The population explosion;

– the list is endless.

Nor does anything he has to say have to be logical responses to questions posed.

Oh no. The academic-pseudo-intellectual version is even more dangerous, who in the face of reality that is more tangible than the massive walls of the slave forts standing along our beaches, still talks of universal truth, universal art, universal literature and the Gross National Product.

Finally, when he has emptied his head of everything, he informs you solemnly that your problem is that you are too young. You must grow up.

Without doubt, the experience is like what a lover of chess or any mind-absorbing sport must feel who goes to a partner's for a game, but discovers he has to play against the dog of the house instead of the master himself.

Yes, my brother,
The worst of them
these days supply local
statistics for those population studies, and
toy with
genocidal formulations.
    That's where the latest crumbs
are being thrown!

It is a long way from home to Europe. A cruel past, a funny present, a major desert or two, a sea, an ocean, several different languages apart, aeroplanes bridge the skies.

Her journey must have had something to do with a people's efforts

'to make good again;'

Because right from the beginning, the embassy had shown a lot of interest.

The minute her name had been submitted, they had come to the campus looking for her in a black Mercedes-Benz, its flag furled.

They had pulled strings for her to obtain her passport in a week instead of three months, and then advised her on the different inoculations to take.

Later, as time shrank for her to leave, the ambassador himself had invited her to his home. The first time to a cocktail party at which it was fairly clear that she was the only insignificant guest, and then to a small dinner in her own honour.

She was to remember that second evening for a long time. It had been full of many things that puzzled her.

The care they must have taken.

The effort they seemed to have made.

She tried very hard to understand why they wanted to go to such trouble.

Crisp table linen.

Glasses and cutlery that shone.

The food, which she instinctively knew was first class in spite of its foreignness, was served from steaming pots.

There was European wine. Her first encounter with that drink.

Who did they think she was?

There had been six of them.

There was the ambassador and his wife

There was another European man who might have been what she was to learn later was the First Secretary, and his wife.

Then there was this African, a single man, her fellow countryman.

She had no idea who he was and did not catch his proper name when they were introduced to each other.

Throughout the evening, they referred to him as Sammy, which was therefore, the only name she could ever associate with him in her mind.

Sammy laughed all the time: even when there was nothing to laugh at. Or when she thought there was nothing to laugh at.

And when he was not laughing loudly, he carried a some-what permanent look of well-being on his face, supported by a fixed smile.

Sammy had obviously been to their country before and seemed to have stayed for a long time. He was very anxious to get her to realise one big fact. That she was unbelievably lucky to have been chosen for the trip. And that, somehow, going to Europe was altogether more like a dress rehearsal for a journey to paradise.

His voice, as he spoke of that far-off land, was wet with longing.

Perhaps he had been invited to the dinner just to sing of the wonders of Europe?

He spoke their language well and was familiar with them in a way that made her feel uneasy.

Our Sister shivered and fidgeted in her chair.

Saliva rose into her mouth every time her eyes fell on her countryman's face.

More saliva rushed into her mouth every time he spoke.

She did not enjoy the food: and the strangeness of it was not the reason.

Time was to bring her many many Sammys. And they always affected her in the same way . . .

On the evening she was leaving, the ambassador and some members of his staff came to the airport to see her off.

Their press officer took pictures of her as she said her farewells.

About a week after she was gone and like a posthumous award, they published her picture in the local newspaper with some information on the trip.

Our Sister had made it.

At the time, many airlines were not allowed to stop at Accra because Johannesburg and other Afrikaaner cities formed a backbone to their African business.

One more Nkrumahn hallucination.

The man was great.

Therefore, Sissie took a plane from Accra to Lagos where she was to join another which would take her to Europe.

It had already arrived from the pit that is South Africa.

Some of us called that land Azania.

Ma-a-ma, ain't no one can laugh at hisself like us.

Besides, when hope dies, what else lives?

As the announcement for departure came, Sissie went on board. She looked at her boarding pass and took the seat indicated on it. It was in the front section of the plane, and by two other seats already occupied by some two Europeans she later learnt were South Africans.

Immediately after they were airborne and instructions had come for them to loosen their belts and feel free to smoke, a neatly coiffured hostess of the airline walked to her. She said, 'You want to join your two friends at the back, yes?'

'My two friends?' wondered Sissie.

She raised her eyes and, following the direction of the hostess's finger, saw two faces. She was about to say she had not met them before . . .

Something told her to cool it.

She went to join them.

Of course, it was a beautiful coincidence that they were two extremely handsome Nigerian men who were going on the same programme she was on.

But to have refused to join them would have created an awkward situation, wouldn't it? Considering too that apart from the air hostess's obviously civilised upbringing, she had been trained to see to the comfort of all her passengers. Naturally, she was only giving Sissie a piece of disinterested advice to make her feel at ease enough to enjoy her flight

The hours of the flight had been organised in such a way that they passed over the bit of Africa left in their way in the dead hours of the night.

So that it was nearly dawn when they crossed the Mediterranean Sea. And as they left Africa, there was this other continent, lighted up with the first streaks of glorious summer sunshine.

Good night Africa. Good morning Europe.

Meanwhile, the moon had been travelling at eye level with them all night. Silent, deathly pale.

Some of us were to wonder at a future date whether the astronauts saw any madness-carrying bugs crawling in millions on rocks that they say have never known heat.

Maybe they didn't notice anything like that.

Not part of operational specifics.

And why should it have been?

It definitely was not to pander to dark superstitious minds that fifty billions were spent!

But just where and when the sun came to chase the moon away, Our Sister thought she heard the music of the spheres.

The Alps at six o'clock in the morning. Grey rocks, more grey rocks. One huge grey rock. . . . Is it really possible that any part of the earth can also reach so high in the sky?

Sissie was overwhelmed, a lowland born. Wondering if this was not the beginning of the world and amoeba yet to be.

She was to wonder the same, many years later in Kenya, as she stood somewhere in the Great Rift Valley, two miles deep in the bowels of the Earth.

Frankfurt. There was an official at the airport to meet them and see that all went smoothly.

From the airport, they took a taxi which drove them into the centre of the city.

The functionary guided them to an eating place where he ordered breakfast for four, including himself.

After they had eaten, they hired another taxi to a railway station. They were going to take a train from there to a small town where they would stay for two weeks and learn to get used to being in a very strange country.

At the station, they learnt that their train would not leave for another hour.

Therefore Sissie felt like strolling around instead of sitting on one spot.

The official was worried. However, Sissie assured him that she would not wander away. There was plenty in the neighbourhood to occupy her. For instance, there seemed to be more shops right inside the station than in the whole of her country. There was no need for her to go outside and get lost.

So she walked along in her gay, gold and leafy brown cloth, looking, feasting her village eyes.

Cloths. Perfume. Flowers. Fruits.·

Then polished steel. Polished tin. Polished brass. Cut glass. Plastic.

As Sissie moved among what was around, saw their shine and their glitter, she told herself that this must be where those 'Consumer Goods' trickled from, to delight so much the hearts of the folks at home. Except that here, there were not only a million times more, but also a thousand times better.

Music. Sounds. Noises.

So many different noises mixed together.

Suddenly, she realised a woman was telling a young girl who must have been her daughter:

'Ja, das Schwartze Mädchen.'

From the little German that she had been advised to study for the trip, she knew that 'das Schwartze Mädchen' meant 'black girl.'

She was somewhat puzzled.

Black girl? Black girl?

So she looked around her, really well this time.

And it hit her. That all that crowd of people going and coming in all sorts of directions had the colour of the pickled pig parts that used to come from foreign places to the markets at home.

Trotters, pig-tails, pig-ears.

She looked and looked at so many of such skins together.

And she wanted to vomit.

Then she was ashamed of her reaction.

Something pulled inside of her.

For the rest of her life, she was to regret this moment

when she was made to notice differences in human colouring.

No matter where she went, what anyone said, what they did. She knew it never mattered.

But what she also came to know was that someone some-where would always see in any kind of difference, an excuse to be mean.

A way to get land, land, more land.

Valleys where green corn would sway in the wind.

A grazing ground for highland cattle.

A stream to guggle the bonnie bairns to sleep.

Gold and silver mines,

Oil

Uranium

Plutonium

Any number of ums –

Clothes to cover skins,

Jewels to adorn,

Houses for shelter, to lie down and sleep.

A harsher edge to a voice.

A sharper ring to commands.

Power, Child, Power.

For this is all anything is about.

Power to decide

Who is to live,

Who is to die,

Where,

When,

How.

The Plums

She was a young mother pushing her baby in a pram. Later, she was to tell Sissie that she did this quite often. She would come and stand where Sissie stood, in the round sentry post, and look at the town and the river.

> There was a castle
> Which the brochure tells you
> Was one of the largest in all
> Germany.
> Germany?
> The land of castles?
> So who was this
> Prince,
> This Lord and Master
> Who had built one of
> The largest castles of them all,
> Possessed the
> Biggest
> Land, the
> Greatest number of
> Serfs?
> And you wondered
> Looking at the river,
> How many
> Virgins had
> Our Sovereign Lord and Master
> Unvirgined on their nuptial nights
> For their young
> Husbands in
> Red-eyed
> Teeth-gnashing
> Agony, their
> Manhoods
> Hurting . . .

But 'all the days are not equal', said the old village wall, and

> The castle is now a youth hostel.

'Are you an Indian?' she asked Sissie.

   'No' she replied –

> Knowing she could be
> Except for the hair.

She might have heard her answer. She might have not. But she was speaking on, the words tumbling out of her mouth as though she had planned out the meeting and even drafted the introductory remarks.

'Yes, I like zem weri much. The Indians. Zey verkt in ze supermarket. Zey ver weri nice.'

'Which Indians?'

'Ze two. It vas before last vinter. For a long time. And zen zey left. I like zem weri much.'

Sissie guessed they might have been male.

> Fact dismissed.
> Two Indians in a small town to house the
> Serfs who
> Slaved for the
> Lord who
> Owned one of the
> Largest castles in all of
> Germany . . .
>
> It is a
> Long way from
> Calcutta to
> Munich:
> Aeroplanes brought you here.
> But what else did
> Migrant birds of the world,
> Beginning with such
> Few feathers too, which
> > drop
> and
> > drop
> and
> > drop
> from
> constant flights and
> > distances?
>
> My

West Indian neighbour and his wife packed up
one morning to go to Canada, saying:
'They say that
Wages
There are quite
Handsome.'
So they went to Liverpool
To wait for a ship
That should have sailed the
Next day. Or so they had thought.
But it came to dock
Months
Later.

Don't
Ask
Me
How they managed with
Two kids.

But
All journeys
End at doorsteps – and
They too
Arrived in Canada,
Where
He, my neighbour,
Died
Soon enough:
Some silly accident in connection with
Underground chambers,
Oxygen supplies and
Computers that took a
Nap . . .
Before the
Contracts were signed.

She – my neighbour's widow,
Planned herself and the kids for a
Distant cousin who
Should have been

Living in
Newark
New Jersey.
'Cept they had not seen one another
In years
Not since
My neighbour's widow left the
Islands to go nursing in
U.K.,
While her
Distant cousin was bound for the
USA,
Where
We all know a
Nigger can make more money than
Any darkie
Anywhere in the
Commonwealth . . .
Yes?

But apart from
Keeping up correspondences with
Nursing distant cousins,
Other duties claim us:
West Indian neighbour's widow
Unknowing
Canadian Pacific
Rolling into
New England
Distant cousin
Gotten shot down . . .
'Any Negro can burn:
Potential snipers all
                    and
Them is all alike.'

The feathers?
They
                    drop
and

                    drop
        and
                    drop, over
        Many
        Seas and
        Lands,
        Until the
        Last wing
                    falls: and
        Skins bared to the
        Cold winds or
        Hot,
        Frozen or
        Scorched,
        We
        Die.

Sissie looked at the young mother and the thought came to
her that

        Here,
        Here on the edge of a pine forest in the
        Heartland of
        Bavaria, among the ruins of one of the
        Largest
        Castles in all
        Germany,
        IT CANNOT BE NORMAL
        for a young
        Hausfrau to
        Like
        Two Indians
        Who work in
        Supermarkets.

        'My Mann is called
                    A D O L F
        And zo is our little zon.'

'Ver do you come from?' she asked Sissie.
    'Ghana.'

'Is that near Canada?'

> Pre-Columbian South American with only a little
> Stretch of imagination
> Perhaps
> But Eskimo?

> No.
> Too wide the
> Disparity
> In
> Skin hue
> Shape of eyes –
> Thanks for the
> Compliment, Madam,
> But
> No.

'I really like ze two Indians who verkt in ze supermarket,' she insisted. 'Zo ver is Ghana?'

'West Africa. The capital is called Accra. It is . . .'

'Ah ja, ja, ja that is ze country zey have ze President Nukurumah, ja?'

'Yes.'

'My name is Marija. But me, I like ze English name Mary. Please call me Mary. Vas is your name?'

'My name? My name is Sissie. But they used to call me Mary too. In school.'

'Mary . . . Mary . . . Mary. Did you say in school zey call you Mary?'

'Yes.'

'Like me?'

'Yes.'

'Vai?'

'I come from a Christian family. It is the name they gave me when they baptised me. It is also good for school and work and being a lady.'

'Mary, Mary . . . and you an African?'

'Yes.'

'But that is a German name!' said Marija.

Mary?
But that is an English name, said Jane.
Maria . . . Marlene.
That is a Swedish name, said Ingrid.
Marie is a French name, said Michelle.
Naturally
Naturellement
Natürlich!

Mary is anybody's name but . . .

Small consolation that in some places,
The patient, long-suffering
Missionaries could not get as far
As
Calling up to the pulpit
A man and his wife who
Fight in the night
and
Whip them
Before the
Whole congregation of the
SAVED.

But my brother,
They got
Far
Enough.

Teaching among other things,
Many other things,
That
For a child to grow up
To be a
Heaven-worthy individual,
He had
To have
Above all, a
Christian name.

And what shall it profit a native that
He should have

Systems to give
A boy
A girl
Two
Three names or
More?
Yaw Mensah Adu Preko Oboroampa Okotoboe

Ow, my brother . . .
Indeed there was a time when
Voices sang
Horns blew
Drums rolled to
Hail
Yaw
    – for getting born on Thursday
Preko.
    – Just to extol Yaw
Mensah
    – Who comes third in a series of males
Adu
    – A name from father
    after venerable ancestor,
Okotoboe
    – For hailing the might of Adu.

No, my brother,
We no more
Care for
Such
Anthropological
Shit:

A man could have
Ten names.
They were all the same –
Pagan
Heathen
Abominable idolatry to the
Hearing of
God,

Who, bless his heart,
Is a rather
Nice
Old
European
Gentleman with a flowing white beard.
. . . And he sits
Flanked on either side by
Angels that take the roll-call for
The Elect.

Lord,
Let us Thy Servants depart in peace
Into our rest
Our oblivion and never
Dare expect
Angels who take roll-calls in
Latin – most likely –
To twist rather delicate tongues
Around names like
– Gyaemehara
Since, dear Lord, Your
Angels, like You, are
Western
White
English, to be precise.
Oh dear visionary Caesar!
There are no other kinds of
Angels, but
Lucifer, poor Black Devil.

Marija was warm.

Too warm for
Bavaria, Germany
From knowledge gained since.

She laughed easily. Her small buck teeth brilliantly white against thin lips flaming red with lipstick.

White teeth –
Used to be one of the

Unfortunate characteristics of
Apes and
Negroes.
All that is
Changed now.
White teeth are in, my brother,
Because Someone is
Making
Money out of
White teeth.

'I like to be your friend, yes?' asked Marija wistfully.

'Yes.'

'And I call you Sissie, . . . please'?

'Sure.'

'Zo vas is zis name, "Sissie"'?

'Oh, it is just a beautiful way they call "Sister" by people who like you very much. Especially if there are not many girl babies in the family . . . one of the very few ways where an original concept from our old ways has been given expression successfully in English.'

'Yes?'

'Yes . . . Though even here, they had to beat in the English word, somehow.'

'Your people, they see many small things about people, yes?'

'Yes. Because a long time ago, people was all people had.'

'Ah zo. And you, you have many brothers and no sisters?'

'No. I mean, it is not like that for me. They call me Sissie because of something else. Some other reason . . . to do with school and being with many boys who treated me like their sister . . .'

'Oh yes?'

'Yes.'

'I really liked zose Indians. I sink of zem weri much as you speak English.'

A common heritage. A
Dubious bargain that left us
Plundered of

Our gold
Our tongue
Our life – while our
Dead fingers clutch
English – a
Doubtful weapon fashioned
Elsewhere to give might to a
Soul that is already
Fled.

ONCE UPON A TIME, she said,
I too had met an Indian
In Göttingen or thereabouts
My feelings were nebulous
Not·liking or liking
Only hearing some other
Friend from some other place:

'We are the victims of our History and our
Present. They place too many obstacles in the
Way of Love. And we cannot enjoy even our
Differences in peace.'

D'accord
D'accord.

My Indian had been in
Germany 'for quite a number of years.'

Clearly for quite a number of
Years too, a Doctor, a
General Dispenser to the
Imaginary ailments of
Surburbia Germania.
I had looked at him
And switched on
Memory's images,
Pieced together from other
Travellers' tales of sick people in
Calcutta.
'Why did you remain
Here?'

'What do you mean?'
'Why did you not go back
Home?'
'Where?'
'Do they need you as a Doctor
Here,
As desperately?'

My voice rising hysterical,
Me on the verge of tears.
'Hm', he grunted,
'One of these Idealistic Ones, heh?'
Me on the defensive,
'Okay,
If I am idealistic
Let me be idealistic!'

'You say you come from
Ghana?'
'Yes!'
'Well,' he said,
Grinning most deliciously,
'There are as many Ghanaian doctors
practising here as there are Indians . . . more
in fact, counting population ratios at home.'

'I know.
I know.'
My foolish fears flowing,
He tut-tutting me.

But wondering at the same time what I would
Have him do.

Me not knowing what to say.
Though having to agree
'Going to work in a
State hospital is
Unnecessary
Slavery . . . '

Unless you are a smart one
Anxious to use

State beds,
State drugs
State time for civilised
Private patients,
Business tycoons,
Other clever public servants
Who only know how to
Lord-it-over the public,
Lodge-brothers and
Classmates,
Just any
Rascal who can pay for
Himself or his
Wife.

'500 for a boy,
400 for a girl.'

Why should it surprise
That it costs a little more
To make a baby boy?

Busy as we are
Building in earnest,
Firm, solid, foundations for
Our zombie dynasties?

But then,
'They would treat a doctor like shit
If they could get away with it.'

And he, my Indian, in a
Social order that
Froze a thousand years gone, would
Starve
Today
Should he 'open a
Private practice
Anywhere at
Home.'

A child-of-God ministering to the
Children-of-God, who, being
God's own babies
Cannot pay for
Medicare, but feed on
Air and the glory of rich men that
Come and go:
Excellent nourishment for the
Soul, no doubt:
Poor feed for the baby.

So, please,
Don't talk to me of the
Brain –
Drain –
Which of us stays in these days?
But those of us who fear
We cannot survive abroad,
One reason or another?

Gambian ophthalmologist in Glasgow
Philippino lung specialist in Boston
Brazilian cancer expert in
Brooklyn or
Basle or
Nancy.
While at home,
Wherever that may be,
Limbs and senses rot
Leaving
Clean hearts to be
Transplanted into
White neighbours' breasts . . .
                And
Peace Troops and other volunteers
Who in their home towns, might not
Get near patients with
Hayfever in league with
Local incompetence
Prepare

> Rare cases for
> Burial . . .

They agreed that Marija would come and collect Sissie from the ex-castle-youth-hostel at about five o'clock the following afternoon, and take her home.

Five o'clock was a good time to plan an outing for. Because usually, Sissie and the other campers returned from the pine nursery around one o'clock or two. By three, they had finished eating their lunch. Fresh potatoes, German goulash, cheese, sauerkraut, fish in some form or other, other food items. And always, three different types of bread: white bread, black bread, rye bread. Tons of butter. Pots of jam. Indeed, portions at each meal were heavy enough to keep a seven foot quarry worker on his feet for a month. All of which was okay by the campers. So that even after a riotous breakfast, each of them had to have one or two mammoth sandwiches for the mid-morning break.

> They stuffed themselves.
> Oh yes:
> Darling teenage pigs from
> Europe
> Africa
> Latin America
> The Middle East –
> Having realised as
> Quickly as only the young can,
> That perhaps here in
> Bavaria,
> By the softly flowing Salz,
> No one needed their work
> Not their brawn, anyway:

Certainly not in any of the ways that Sissie had known of, as a member of INVOLOU:

> Helping with missionary sense of gratification,
> A village build a school block,
> Dig a new-fangled well
> Straighten a

seventh rate feeder road into a
second rate feeder road . . .

And when you pass by,
Years later,
A warmth creeping inside your chest
As you see a new
Market
Where you had shared the
Unevenly cooked –
Hardly sufficient –
Meatless
Jolof rice.

From all around the Third World,
You hear the same story;
Rulers
Asleep to all things at
All times –
Conscious only of
Riches, which they gather in a
Coma –
Intravenously –

So that
You wouldn't know they were
Feeding if it was not for the
Occasional
Tell-tale trickle somewhere
Around the mouth.
And when they are jolted awake,
They stare about them with
Unseeing eyes, just
Sleepwalkers in a nightmare.

Therefore,
Nothing gets done in
Villages or towns,
If
There are no volunteers,
Local and half-hearted.

There are some other kinds:
Imported,
Eager,
Sweet foreign aid
Eventually to take a
Thousand
For every horse-power put in.

Sissie and her companions were required to be there, eating, laughing, singing, sleeping and eating. Above all eating.

So
They stuffed themselves
With a certain calmness
That passeth all understanding.

They felt no need to worry over who should want them to be there eating. Why should they? Even if the world is rough, it's still fine to get paid to have an orgasm . . . or isn't it? Of course, later on when we have become

Diplomats
Visiting Professors
Local experts in sensitive areas
Or
Some such hustlers,

We would have lost even this small awareness, that in the first place, an invitation was sent . . .

Meanwhile, all that Sissie and her fellow campers had to do by way of work was at a pine nursery; to cover up the bases and stems of pine seedlings with ground turf or peat. To protect them from the coming chill of winter. As the boys shovelled up the turf and wheeled it down in barrows, the girls did the sprinkling.

There were Bavarian peasants too in the garden. Middle-aged woman. At the beginning, the campers could not place them. Then they realised that they were in the employment of some public authority and that in fact it was their work the campers were doing. This peating-up of the little pines had some of the campers feeling bad. Especially the European kids. Unused as they were to being useful in their middle class homes, they had become international volunteers in the hope of getting to the poverty-stricken multitudes of the earth. Rotten luck, there had been friends of theirs who couldn't even leave home. Too many applications. For some time, a few had been made to believe they would get to at least, southern Italy. But now here they were, in southern Germany, nursing prospective Christmas trees!

The Bavarian dames came every day to supervise the work the campers were doing. Or more correctly, just to be with them, around them, chat them up. And when they felt '*die schönenkinder*' were taking the job too seriously, they would move up and pat each of them in turn, asking them to go slow. They probably knew for a fact what the campers could only guess at: that all that to-do was just an excuse to procure the voices of the children of the world to ring carefree through the old forests.

> After
> Each shocking experience
> Mother Earth recovers –
> That, of course is true,
> But, with some effort
> Battered as she is.
> It is not bad if we help her
> Some of the time.

The Bavarian ladies wore black: each one of them, each day.

> Widows
> Widows
> Widows all –
> From knowledge gained since.
> The blood of their young men was
> Needed to mix the concrete for
> Building the walls of
> The Third Reich. But
> Its foundations collapsed before the walls
> were completed.
> Dear Lord,
> Dear Lord,

How this reminds me of the
Abome kings of Dahomey.

That's why
They wonder,
They wonder if, should they
Stop cultivating the little pine trees, would
Something else,
Sown there,
Many many years ago,
In
Those Bavarian woods
           SPROUT?

Marija went for Sissie and took her home, which turned out
to be at the other end of the village. The house, a dainty
new cottage, was the last in a row of several dainty new
cottages, beautifully covered up by their summer foliage of
creepers.

Like the rest, it had a backyard garden where Sissie saw
several kinds of vegetables thriving. She recognised an old
old friend. Tomato. Though in all their uniformity and
richness, those tomatoes looked .like some strange exotic
fruits. Lush, crimson, perfected.

Anyhow, there were real fruit trees in the garden. Sissie
asked Marija to walk around with her while she tried to
identify apples, pears, plums, with her mind thrown back
to textbook illustrations at home:

           Known landscapes
           Familiar territories
           Pampas of Australia
           Steppes of Eurasia
           Prairies of America
           Koumis
           Conifers
           Snow.

           Though outside in the African sun,
           Giant trees stood for centuries and
           Little plants

> Bloomed and
> Died,
> All unmentioned in
> Geography notes.

They went indoors, sat down, chattered about this and that, then finally had coffee with cookies.

Marija was reluctant to let Sissie leave early. She told her that Big Adolf's shift ran the whole day and half the night. Therefore, there was no need to cook supper. She could scrounge up a small meal which the two of them would eat together. There was plenty of cheese, sausages, fruits, and yes, yes, some cold flesh . . .

'Flesh?'

> 'Meat, yes?'
> 'Ah so . . .'

Yes, Big Adolf would come home certainly, but late, very late, and so tired he would not eat. They had not finished paying for the dainty new cottage, Marija informed Sissie, so Big Adolf had to do overtime, much overtime.

When Sissie managed to convince Marija that she had to return to the youth hostel, Marija immediately produced two brown paperbags filled with apples, pears, tomatoes, and plums.

> But
> The plums.
> What plums.
> Such plums.

Sissie had never seen plums before she came to Germany. No, she had never seen real, living, plums. Stewed prunes, yes. Dried, stewed, sugared-up canned plums . . .

> Praise the Lord for all dead things.

> First course:
> Cream of asparagus soup
> Thirty months in an aluminium
> Tin.

Second course:
Chicken moriturus under
Pre-mixed curry from
Shepherds Bush:
And since we are learning to take
Desserts – true mark of a leisured class –
Canned prunes
Canned pears
Canned apples
Apricots
Cherries.

Brother,
The internal logic is super-cool:
The only way to end up a cultural
Vulture
Is to feed on carrion all the way

You cannot achieve the
Moribund objectives of a
Dangerous education by using
Living forces.
Therefore, since
'Ghosts know their numbers,'
Dr. Intellectual Stillborn
– with perfect reason –
Can break his neck to recruit
Academic corpses from Europe.
Wraith-like with age or
Just plain common.

Like pears, apricots and other fruits of the Mediterranean
and temperate zones, Sissie had seen plums for the first
time in her life only in Frankfurt. In the next few weeks, she
was to see lots of them wherever she went, through the length
and breadth of Germany. It was midsummer and the fruit
stalls were overflowing. She had decided that being fruits,
she liked them all, although her two loves were going to be
pears and plums. And on those two she gorged herself. So
she had good reason to feel fascinated by the character of

Marija's plums. They were of a size, sheen and succulence she had not encountered anywhere else in those foreign lands. And which, unknown to her then, she would not be encountering again. What she was also not aware of, though, was that those Bavarian plums owed their glory in her eyes and on her tongue not only to that beautiful and black Bavarian soil, but also to other qualities that she herself possessed at that material time:

> Youthfulness
> Peace of mind
> Feeling free:
> Knowing you are a rare article,
> Being
> Loved.

So she sat, Our Sister, her tongue caressing the plump berries with skin-colour almost like her own, while Marija told her how she had selected them specially for her, off the single tree in the garden.

During the days that followed, Marija came to the castle every afternoon at five o'clock to take Sissie out. They avoided the main street and took a path through a park where they walked Little Adolf for a while before getting home. Sometimes they sat and talked. Or rather, Marija asked a few questions while Sissie, answering, told her friend about her

> Mad country and her
> Madder continent.

At other times, they just sat, each with her own thoughts. Occasionally, one of them would look up at the other. If their eyes met, they would smile. At the end of each day, she returned to the castle later than she had done the previous evening. And more heavily loaded too. For there was always a couple of brown paper bags, filled with delicacies, fruits and plums. Always, there were the plums. Sissie realised that Marija picked each lot about twenty-four hours ahead and kept them overnight in a polythene bag; a process that softened the plums and also rid them of their fresh tangy taste, preserving a soothing sweetness.

Yes,
Work is love made visible.

And so it was that Our Sister became known to her fellow campers in the ex-castle youth hostel as The-Bringer-of-Goodies-After-Lights-out.

Supper was at seven. And what with the quantity of it, its overall density and nothing active to do afterwards but singing songs and rapping, most of the campers were ready to retire early to bed. Except that the environment was a sure sleep-breaker. For who knows of a better inspirer of puppy-love, European-style, than

An ancient ruined castle at the edge of a
Brooding pine forest, on the
Bank of a soft flowing river that
Sparkles silver
Under the late-night
Sun?

So there was a great deal of hand-holding, wet-kissing along ancient cobbled corridors. Pensive stares at the silvery eddies of the river.

The promises exchanged were not going to be kept. But who cared?

Love is always better when
Doomed . . .
If Sonja Simonian, Jewish,
Second generation immigrant from
Armenia to Jerusalem
Falls in love with Ahmed Mahmoud bin
Jabir from Algeria –
Then who dares to
Hope? Or not to hope?

On others, the great romanticism in the setting was completely lost. Most of Sissie's room-mates were such infants. However, even they stayed up. They might get into their bunks, but they played pillows, waiting for her to return, an hour or so before midnight. Nor was this surprising, it being midsummer and the day so long.

As soon as they heard the sound of her approaching figure, they would leap off their beds as one of their voices yelled: 'The plums!'

Screaming and yelping like baby hounds, they would jump on her, seize on the inevitable brown paper bags and devour their contents. And no one could go to sleep until the last plum had vanished.

There was Gertie from Bonn, free, light Gertie . . .

Jayne from East Putney, London, whose mother killed Sissie with

        'Deeah, Jayn's been awai all dai,' . . .

Our Sister whose British-born and British-trained teachers had spent hours moulding her tongue around the nooks and crannies of the Received Pronunciation . . .

Marilyn. She took Sissie to visit her teacher training college one evening. Somewhere in the suburbs of London. And the first thing she did was to point out for Sissie the only black girl on campus. Triumph written over her face.

      It happens all the time.

      At nine a showpiece
      At eighteen a darling
      What shall you be
      At thirty?
      A dog among the masters, the
      Most masterly of the
      Dogs.

      Father is the Minister of Education
      At home. He knows where to get
      Quality, so for
      Education and other
      Essentials, he orders straight from
      Europe. And it's really
      Better if we go
      There for it.

> Enrolled us at
> Six months old,
> You cannot rescue too early, you know . . .

Sissie in Lower Bavaria was something of a crowd-getter. It seemed as if any open function that was organised for the volunteers became an automatic success if she was present.

Since for those natives, the mere fact of the presence of the African girl was phenomenal.

Some among them had come across blacks on rare trips to Munich. Blacks who, whether they were American soldiers from NATO military bases or African students, always turned out to be men and fairly fluent speakers of German. And therefore not so exotic.

Whereas Our Sister was not only a female, but also spoke no German. They had heard she was fluent in English. That made no difference. English might be a familiar language but they neither spoke it nor understood it when it was spoken.

As for the African Miss, ah . . . h . . . h . . . look at her costume. How charming. And they gaped at her, pointing at her smile. Her nose. Her lips. Their own eyes shining. Not expecting her to feel embarrassed.

> That's why, my brother,
> You and I
> Shall be
> Impressed with
> Aeronautics and all such
> Acrobatics when they
> Bring us a
> Breathing Martian or a
> Ten-eyed
> Hairy drummer from the
> Moon . . .

Meanwhile who was this Marija Sommer who was monopolising the curiosity that provided such fun just by being? A little housewife married to a factory hand?

And they fumed.

They raged. The thinned-out-end of the old aristocracy and those traditional lickers of aristocratic arse, the pastor, the burgomaster and the schoolteacher . . . Joined by the latest newly-arrived.

The earliest of the new people had come in with the pre-war National Construction that had expanded the size of the ancient village. For in those pine forests, they say the Leader had had built one of those massive chemical plants that served the Empire. They say that in the very very big laboratories of the chemical plant, experiments were done on herb, animal and man. But especially on man, just hearing of which should get a grown-up man urinating on himself, while seeing anything of them should keep him screaming in his sleep for at least one year.

After the war, they converted the structure into just another chemical plant for producing pain-killing drugs. And more people came into the village. And with the people the social services, and their bosses. Most of these bosses, especially those who had anything to do with money, considered themselves important enough to be in the limelight.

So how was it that it was not them or their wives escorting the African Miss? There must be something wrong with that Marija Sommer! !

Why does she always walk with the black girl? asked the director of the local branch of a bank.

Sommer does not speak English and the African speaks no German. So who interprets for them? asked the manager of a supermarket.

What could they be talking about? wondered an insurance broker.

She must not take her to her house every day!

She must be getting neurotic!

It is perverse.

SOMEONE MUST TELL HER HUSBAND! !

And Marija's neighbours suddenly became important. For was it not they who were near the drama? And for once in their lives their afternoons were filled with meaning, as they sat and spied on the goings on between the two. A group of them would invariably find a reason to come and see

Marija any time they knew Sissie was in, and yet pretend it was not because of her they came. Then hiding behind their language, they would slug Marija with questions, hang around for much more time than was reasonable in even their own eyes, and eventually leaving them alone, only when they sensed it would be too much to stay any longer.

Meanwhile Marija could tell Sissie of people whom she did not remember vaguely as ever meeting at all, now greeting her on the street and often stopping to ask her rather familiar questions as though they were life-long friends. Marija was always calm.

But something of the commotion reached Marija so that the two women finally agreed to push up their meetings a couple of hours late.

That improved matters somewhat. Darkness did not come early, it being summer and the day so long. Yet by the normal hours of the evening, the creature man had responded to the workings of his body and succumbed to a feeling of tiredness. By eight o'clock, day activities had ended, giving way to those of night. The main street was deserted and the eerie quietness characteristic of night had enveloped human dwellings, even though the sun shone.

There was a certain strangeness about Marija the first time she came to fetch Sissie in the evening. Her eyes had a gleam in them that the African girl would have found unsettling if the smile that always seemed to be dancing around her lips had also not been more obviously there. She was flushed and hot. Sissie could feel the heat.

And there had always been formalities to go through before Sissie could leave the hostel. Like looking for one of the camp leaders to tell them she was going out. And also booking out, at the reception desk.

That evening, things turned out to be a little more difficult than usual. The camp leader thought it was rather late and the receptionist stated flatly that going out that late was against the rules.

Sissie stood and looked wistful, while Marija pleaded with them in their language and succeeded only in irritating them even more.

The receptionist was immovable. In the end, the camp leader gave in and then reluctantly explained to the receptionist that in spite of the rules, they obviously could not refuse the African Miss anything.

Outside, Marija heaved a sigh of relief declaring that she would not have been able to bear it if they had prevented Sissie from accompanying her home.

As for Our Sister, she didn't comment on that. What she was thinking was that the situation did not call for such panic. For as far as she was concerned, she could have gone back to her companions, after fixing an earlier date for the next day.

'I am zo glad vee are going home tonight, Sissie,' insisted Marija.

'I am too,' Sissie agreed.

A cool breeze was blowing. The river was a dark grey in the somewhat twilight and lapping quietly against the stone and concrete embankment. It was one of these moments in time when one feels secure, as though all of reality is made up of what can be seen, smelt, touched and explained.

'Sissie,' began Marija, with that special way she had for pronouncing the name. As though she was consciously making an effort to get the music in it not to die too soon but rather carry on into far distances.

'Yes, Marija?' she responded.

'I have baked a cake for you.'

'M-m-m,' Our Sister cooed; pretending to be more delighted at the news than she actually felt.

Indeed she was feeling uncomfortable.

She had already added about ten pounds to her weight since she arrived in that country. Therefore, she was no longer capable of feeling ecstasy at the news that any type of cake had been baked in her honour. Even if she was only an unconscious African schoolgirl?

> Who does not know that
> Plumpness and
> Ugliness are the

Same, an
Invitation for
Coronary something or other?
That
Carbohydrates are debilitating
Anyhow?

Besides, my sister,
If you want to believe the
Brothers
Telling
You
How Fat they
Like their
Women,
Think of the
Shapes of the ones they
Marry;

How
Thin

How
Stringy
Thin.

'It is a plum cake,' pursued Marija.

'Ah-h-h.' Our Sister cried softly. In anguish. For did she not remember that the cakes the natives of the land baked were very sweet and she herself did not like too many sweet things?

They walked on. Happy then, just to be alive. But soon, they came across an old man and an old woman, who stopped dead in their tracks. Two pairs of eyes popping out of their sockets. Old man talking his language; plenty of words: pointing first to his arm then to Sissie's arm, then to his, then to hers, back to his own arm then again to Sissie's arm. Poor old man breathing heavily and sweating. Old woman anxiously speaking her language. Plenty of words. Marija smiling, smiling, smiling. Sissie asking Marija for explanation of what is happening. Marija

blushing R-E-D. Marija blushing but refusing to answer
Sissie's question.

> Yes, my sister,
> Some things that
> Really
> Happen to us in our wanderings are
> Funnier than
> Travel jokes.

They walked on. Along the main thoroughfare of the town.
Now their inner joys gone, too aware of the sad ways of man.
  Who was Marija Sommer?

> A daughter of mankind's
> Self-appointed most royal line,
> The House of Aryan –
>
> An heiress to some
> Legacy that would make you
> Bow
> Down
> Your head in
> Shame and
> Cry.

And Our Sister?

> A Little
> Black
> Woman who
> If things were what they should have been,
> And time had not a way of
> Making nonsense of Man's
> Dreams, would
> Not
> Have been
> There
> Walking
> Where the
> Führer's feet had trod –
> A-C-H-T-U-N-G !

48

They arrived at Marija's house. Just then Sissie realised that Little Adolf had not been with them.

'Where is Little Adolf, Marija?'

'He is in the house, sleeping . . .'

'Of course, of course,' said Sissie to herself. She had forgotten that it was much later than any safe hour to take a baby out. Marija was still talking.

'I wanted to be alone. To talk with you . . . you know, Sissie, sometimes one wants to be alone. Even from the child one loves so much. Just for a very little time . . . may be?'

She finished uncertainly, looking up to Sissie who did not have a child, as if for confirmation. A reassurance. That she was not speaking blasphemy.

> It is
> Heresy
>
> In
> Africa
> Europe,
> Everywhere.
>
> This is
> Not a statement to come from a
> Good mother's lips –
>
> Touch wood.

Sissie was silent. Thinking that she did not know about babies. But then, wasn't Marija too often by herself anyway?

> Yet
> Who also said that
> Being alone is not like
> Being
> Alone?

They entered the house. It was as usual, very quiet. They turned from the doorway into the kitchen which seemed to serve also as the family sitting room. It was large and comfortable.

'Sit down, Sissie.'

The chairs were modernistic affairs in artificial fibre. And two of them were placed companionably together as though Marija had planned it that way. Sissie sat in one of them.

Marija relieved her of the sweater which she had taken along with her although the day had been very warm. For it seemed not to matter to Our Sister how warm the days were. She could never trust this weather that changed so often and so violently, used as she was to the eternal promise of tropical warmth.

Marija wondered if Sissie was ready for coffee.

Sissie said no, not for a little while. But was there water? Sissie had noticed that for some reason, a request for water always drew gasps from her hosts and hostesses; it didn't make a difference in which part of the land they were. At any rate, they appeared never to drink any water themselves.

'Yes,' said Marija, 'but perhaps black currant juice?'

They grew in her mother's garden. The black currants did. Plenty, plenty. And every summer since she was little, her one pleasure had been preserving black currants – making its jam, bottling its juices. And she still went home to help. Or rather, she went to avail herself of the pleasure, the beauty, the happiness at harvest time: of being with many people, the family. Working with a group. If they had met earlier, she could have taken Sissie home for that year's harvest. It was not far away. Her home. She was sure her mother would have liked Sissie very much.

Sissie was sipping the good drink . . . Marija asked her if she would like to see Little Adolf. Sissie said yes, getting up. But Marija said she could finish her drink. Later, they would go upstairs to see Little Adolf and Sissie would like to be shown around the upstairs of the house, since they had so far always remained downstairs?

Sissie agreed. Then she went on to say how beautiful she thought he was. The mother smiled, delighted. She had already informed Sissie that Adolf was going to be her only child. There had been complications with his birth and the Herr Doktor had advised her not to attempt to have another child. It might be unsafe for her. And now smiling even more broadly, she said that since Adolf was going to be the only child, she was very happy he was a boy.

Any good woman
In her senses
With her choices
Would say the
Same

In Asia
Europe
Anywhere:

For
Here under the sun,
Being a woman
Has not
Is not
Cannot
Never will be a
Child's game

From knowledge gained since –

So why wish a curse on your child
Desiring her to be female
?
Beside, my sister,
The ranks of the wretched are
Full,
Are full.

Now Marija was saying that she was, oh so very, sorry, that she had no hope of ever visiting Sissie in Africa. But she prayed that one day, Little Adolf would go there, maybe.

And there is always
SOUTH AFRICA
and
RHODESIA,
you see.

'Sissie?'

'Yes, Marija?'

'You are from Africa. And oh, that is vonderful. Weri vunderbar. And you trawel so much. But ver also did you say you vent?'

'Nigeria.'

'Oh yes?'

'Yes.'

'Neegeria. Ah-h, Nee-ge-ria. Vas did you go to do in Neegeria?'

Sissie opened her mouth to answer her. But it appeared there was something else Marija wanted to know first.

'Nee-ge-ria. What is Neegeria like?'

'Oh like my country. Only bigger. Or rather it has got bigger, everything that my country has.'

Sissie told Marija that she always persuaded friends from abroad who could only visit one country in Africa to make sure they went to Nigeria.

Marija was shocked because Sissie was sounding un-patriotic.

'Why, Sissie?'

Our Sister tried to explain herself. That as far as she was concerned, Nigeria not only has all the characteristics which nearly every African country has, but also presents these characteristics in bolder outlines. Therefore, what is the point in persuading a friend to see the miniature version of anything when the real stuff is there?

Nigeria.
Nigeria our love
Nigeria our grief.
Of Africa's offspring
Her likeness –

O Nigeria.
More of everything we all are,
More of our heat
   Our naiveté
   Our humanity
   Our beastliness

Our ugliness
Our wealth
Our beauty

A big mirror to
Our problems
Our tragedies.
Our glories.
Mon ami,
Household quarrels of
Africa become a
WAR in
Nigeria:

'And Ghana?'
'Ghana?'

Ghana?
Just a
Tiny piece of beautiful territory in
Africa – had
Greatness thrust upon her
Once.
But she had eyes that saw not –
That was a long time ago . . .
Now she picks tiny bits of
Undigested food from the
Offal of the industrial world . . .
O Ghana.

Sissie shivered.
'What is it?'
'I am feeling cold.'
'I bring you the sweater, yes?'
'No, it is not the air that makes me cold. I shall feel better soon.'
'Anywhere else you have been in Africa?'
'Yes.'
'Where?'
'Upper Volta . . .'
'And where is Upper Wolta?'

'On top of Ghana.'
'What did you go to do?'
'Tourism.'
Marija laughed.
   Was Upper Wolta also beautiful?
   'Yes,' said Sissie. 'But in a poorer, drier, sadder way.'
   'Ja?'
   'Ja.'

She did not know she thought so then.
She was to know.

The bible talks of
Wilderness
Take your eyes to see
Upper Volta, my brother –
Dry land. Thorn trees. Stones.

The road from the Ghana border to
Ouagadougou was
Out-of-sight!

The French, with
Characteristic contempt and
Almost
Childish sense of
Perfidy had
A long time ago, tarred two
Narrow
Strips of earth for motor vehicles.
Each wide enough for
One tyre.

Result: When two vehicles passed one another,
both of them had to get off the tarred strips and on to the
dust and stones, or mud and stones according to the time of
year. Three friends travelled on it at a time when there was
no difference between the strips and the rest. The former
being full of deathly potholes and the latter just one long
ditch. As they sped along, the car fell into a pothole and
caught fire. They were saved by their fates. For between

the three of them they had only enough knowledge about automobiles to remove and fix a tyre after a puncture, and no more. But groping around blindly in the smoke, the smartest among them snapped some wires and the smoking stopped. It was in the middle of nowhere and so all they could do was sit by the roadside and wait for help. Presently a Frenchman came by. The friends asked him why the country permitted its international road to remain in such condition years after independence.

'The President himself uses it every day.' The Frenchman said, shrugged his shoulders and drove off.

> A sickening familiar tale.
> Poor Upper Volta too.
>
> There are
> Richer, much
> Richer countries on this continent
> Where
> Graver national problems
> Stay
> Unseen while
> Big men live their
> Big lives
> Within . . .

At the end of the day, the three friends came to a tiny French provincial town called Ouagadougou. Where between the heat of the Sahara and the heat of the Equator, they hang out cotton wool on window sills for snow, it being the Feast of Noel.

> We have heard too,
> Have we not? Of countries in
> Africa where
> Wives of
> Presidents hail from
> Europe.
> Bringing their brothers or . . . who knows?
> To run the
> Economy.

Excellent idea . . .
How can a
Nigger rule well
Unless his
Balls and purse are
Clutched in
Expert White Hands?

And the Presidents and their
First Ladies
Govern from the North
Provence, Geneva, Milan . . .
Coming south to Africa
Once a year
For holidays.

Meanwhile,
Look!

In the capitals,
Ex-convicts from European
Prisons drive the city buses, and
Black construction workers
Sweat under the tropical sun, making
Ice-skating rinks for
The Beautiful People . . .
While other Niggers sit
With vacant stares
          Or
Busy, spitting their lungs out.

JUST LIKE THE GOOD OLD DAYS
BEFORE INDEPENDENCE

Except –
The present is
S-o-o-o much
Better!
For
In these glorious times when
Tubercular illiterates

Drag yams out of the earth with
Bleeding hands,

Champagne sipping
Ministers and commissioners
Sign away
Mineral and timber
Concessions, in exchange for
Yellow wheat which
The people can't eat.

And at noon,
The wives drive Mercedes-Benzes to
Hairdressers', making ready for
The evening's occasion
While on the market place,
The good yams rot for
Lack of transportation and
The few that move on,
Are shipped for
Paltry cents –
To foreign places as
Pretty decorations
On luxury tables.

We must sing and dance
Because some Africans made it.

EDUCATION HAS BECOME TOO
EXPENSIVE. THE COUNTRY CANNOT
AFFORD IT FOR EVERYBODY.
Dear Lord,
So what can we do about
Children not going to school,

When
Our representatives and interpreters,
The low-achieving academics
In low profile politics
Have the time of their lives
Grinning at cocktail parties and around
Conference tables?

At least, they made it, didn't they?

No,
Man does not live by
Gari or ugali alone –

Therefore
We do not complain about
Expensive trips to
Foreign 'Varsities' where
Honorary doctorate degrees
Come with afternoon teas and
Mouldy Saxon cakes from
Mouldier Saxon dames . . .

Nor do we mind
That when they come back here
Having mortgaged the country for a
Thousand and a year
To maintain themselves on our backs
With capitalist ships and fascist planes,
They
Tell
Us
How the water from their
Shit-bowls
Is better than what the villagers
Drink . . .

Ow, glory.
While
Able-bodied fishermen
Disappear in
Cholera, the rest, from under
Leaking roofs and unlit alleys
Shall drum,
and sing
dance
with
joy

This year of the pig-iron anniversary

Because
There is ecstasy
In dying from the hands of a
Brother
Who
Made
It.

. . . .

Now we hear the road is
First class to Ouagadougou
Done-up with borrowed money from
Those who know where to sow
     – even in a wilderness –
To reap a millionfold.

'And now you come to Germany?' asked Marija.
     'Yes,' our sister answered.
     But before Bavaria, there had been France, Belgium,
The Netherlands. One day in Salzburg, six in the two
Berlins.

West Berlin –
As loud as a
Self-conscious whore at a
Gay last-night party
Aboard a sinking ship
East Berlin,
Quiet like a haunted house
On a Sunday afternoon.

With her neutral tastes, Sissie disliked both.
     'Sissie, who pays for all the trawel?'
     'Marija, there was a time when it was fashionable to be
African. And it paid to be an African student. And if you
were an African student with the wanderlust, you travelled.'

Young Christian Movements
Young Muslim Movements,
The Non-Believers' Conferences for Youth,
The Co-ordinated Committees for Students
of The Free World,

The First Internationals for Socialist Youth,
International Workcamping for
Non-Aligned Students . . .

'It is money well-spent.
Nobody's fault that they do not know
How to make use of their
Staggering natural resources.

But first!

Their leaders must be wooed
For now and tomorrow.

And, it's quite in order
To procure
One
Or two of their sable countenances,
To garnish dull speeches and resolutions –

We
Know
What
We
Want:
The airlines profit a little too.'

And some of us paused and wondered
How long it would all last.

Marija's eyes were red. She was saying that since she had
met Sissie, she had been wishing she was better educated
to go places . . . Not just like any tourist. Sissie said she was
sorry. Not wanting pity, Marija smiled, saying it was good
to have Little Adolf who would go to university, travel and
come back to tell her all about his journeys.

'Yes,' said Sissie.

Remembering her own mother,
To whom she sent
Shamefully
Expurgated versions of
Her travel tales.

> Letters?
> Once a trip, even if a trip lasts
> A lifetime.

They sat and time crept on. The false dusk had given way to proper night. Darkness had brought her gifts of silence and heaviness, making the most carefree of us wonder, when we are alone, about our place in all this.

Sissie had been unconsciously looking down, unaware that Marija had been watching her all the time. When Sissie lifted her head and their eyes met, red blood rushed into Marija's face. So deeply red.

Sissie felt embarrassed for no reason that she knew. The atmosphere changed.

Once or so, at the beginning of their friendship, Sissie had thought, while they walked in the park, of what a delicious love affair she and Marija would have had if one of them had been a man.

Especially if she, Sissie had been a man. She had imagined and savoured the tears, their anguish at knowing that their love was doomed. But they would make promises to each other which of course would not stand a chance of getting fulfilled. She could see Marija's tears . . .

That was a game. A game in which one day, she became so absorbed, she forgot who she was, and the fact that she was a woman. In her imagination, she was one of these black boys in one of these involvements with white girls in Europe. Struck by some of the stories she had heard, she shivered, absolutely horrified.

> First Law:
> The Guest Shall Not Eat Palm-Nut Soup.
> Too intimate, too heavy.
>
> But my brothers do not know,
> Or knowing, forget.
>
> Yes?
>
> There are
> 'Exceptions

Beautiful exceptions,
Wonderful success?

But the rest?

I wail for
Lost Black minds
-- Any lost Black mind --
Because
A tailor for the poor
Can ill afford to throw away his
Scraps:

Beautiful Black Bodies
Changed into elephant-grey corpses,
Littered all over the western world,
Thrown across railway tracks for
midnight expresses to mangle
just a little bit more --
Offered to cold flowing water
Buried in thickets and snow
Their penises cut.

Marija said quietly, 'You shall eat now, Sissie?'

'No. Marija, I am not hungry. It is very late, I think I should go back.'

'Me, I am also not hungry. But you said you want to look at Little Adolf, yes? And I also show you the upstairs of the house?'

'Okay,' said Sissie, slowly coming out of her misery into a world where the need to pay mortgages and go on holidays kept married chambers empty for strangers' inspection.

Both of them stood up and stretched. As they went up the stairs, all images of twentieth century modernia escaped Sissie. Rather, what with the time of night, it seemed to her as though she was moving, not up, but down into some primeval cave. A turn to the right, a turn to the left, one more to the right, behold.

Sissie whistled.

'She is a bitch
Or a witch
Who whistles' the old ones had said.

Sissie whistled.

Displeasing gods she did not
Know – only heard of.

The room indeed looked as if it was cut out of a giant rock
that must have existed in the architect's mind. All triangles
and disappearing corners. White walls. A giant white bed,
laid out smooth, waiting to be used.

Speak softly
Tread lightly
It is a holy place
A sanctuary for shrouded dreams.

Indeed, Sissie was convinced she had no right to be there.
And Marija? Sissie could not associate her with the deserted
looking chamber or its simple funereal elegance. And anyway, there she was, moving silently about, that strange
Marija, touching this, touching that, as though for her too
this was a first visit to the room.

On either side of the bed was a little chest. On one,
there was nothing. On the other was one book, a handker-
chief . . . Directly facing the bed was a built-in dressing
table, a crescent-shaped shelf which projected out of the
wall, making that side of the room look like a bar. On this
shelf were bottled affairs from the beauty business. Fragile
weapons for a ferocious war. There they stood, tall and
elegant with slender necks and copious bottoms, their tops
glittering golden over bodies that exuded delicate femaleness
in their pastel delicacy. Pink and blue creams. More pink
and blue lotions. Skin foods that were milky white or
avocado green proclaiming impressive scientific origins.

There were some of them of whose uses Sissie did not have
the vaguest idea. They all looked expensive. Yet with a
number of them also still in their packaging, nothing looked
over-used.

Sissie felt Marija's cold fingers on her breast. The fingers of Marija's hand touched the skin of Sissie's breasts while her other hand groped round and round Sissie's midriff, searching for something to hold on to.

It was the left hand that woke her up to the reality of Marija's embrace. The warmth of her tears on her neck. The hotness of her lips against hers.

As one does from a bad dream, impulsively, Sissie shook herself free. With too much effort, unnecessarily, so that she unintentionally hit Marija on the right cheek with the back of her right hand.

It all happened within a second. Two people staring at one another. Two mouths wide open with disbelief.

Sissie thought of home. To the time when she was a child in the village. Of how she always liked to be sleeping in the bedchamber when it rained, her body completely-wrapped-up in one of her mother's akatado-cloths while mother herself pounded fufu in the anteroom which also served as a kitchen when it rained. Oo, to be wrapped up in mother's cloth while it rained. Every time it rained.

And now where was she? How did she get there? What strings, pulled by whom, drew her into those pinelands where not so long ago human beings stoked their own funeral pyres with other human beings, where now a young Aryan housewife kisses a young black woman with such desperation, right in the middle of her own nuptial chamber, with its lower middle-class cosiness? A love-nest in an attic that seems to be only a nest now, with love gone into mortgage and holiday hopes?

Marija's voice came from far away, thin, tremulous and full of old tears.

'This is our bedroom. Big Adolf and I.'

> Who is Big Adolf?
> What does he look like?
> Big Adolf, the father of Little Adolf,
> Naturally.

But then how can one believe in the existence of this being? You make friends with a woman. Any woman. And she has a child. And you visit the house. Invited by the woman certainly. Every evening for many days. And you stay many hours on each occasion but you still never see the husband and one evening the woman seizes you in her embrace, her cold fingers on your breasts, warm tears on your face, hot lips on your lips, do you go back to your village in Africa and say ... what do you say even from the beginning of your story that you met a married woman? No, it would not be easy to talk of this white woman to just anyone at home ... Look at how pale she suddenly is as she moves shakily, looking lost in her own house?

Marija was crying silently. There was a tear streaming out of one of her eyes. The tear was coming out of the left eye only. The right eye was completely dry. Sissie felt pain at the sight of that one tear. That forever tear out of one eye. Suddenly Sissie knew. She saw it once and was never to forget it. She saw against the background of the thick smoke that was like a rain cloud over the chimneys of Europe,

L
O
N
E
L
I
N
E
S
S

Forever falling like a tear out of a woman's eye.

And so this was it?
Bullying slavers and slave-traders.
Solitary discoverers.
Swamp-crossers and lion hunters.
Missionaries who risked the cannibal's pot to bring the world to the heathen hordes.

Speculators in gold in diamond uranium and copper

Oil you do not even mention –
Preachers of apartheid and zealous educators.
Keepers of Imperial Peace and homicidal
plantation owners.
Monsieur Commandant and Madame the
Commandant's wife.
Miserable rascals and wretched whores whose
only distinction in life was that at least they were better
than the Natives . . .

As the room began to spin around her, Sissie knew that
she had to stop herself from crying. Why weep for them?
In fact, stronger in her was the desire to ask somebody why
the entire world has had to pay so much and is still paying
so much for some folks' unhappiness. There it was. Still
falling.

Once upon a time, many years ago, a missionary went to
the Guinea coast. Not to find some of the legendary gold
dust that made the sands on the shores glitter. Perhaps not.
But to be headmistress of a girls' school . . . In the course
of time, they say she turned into a panting tigress whose
huge bosoms never suckled a cub. She gave first her youth,
then the rest of her life, to educating and straightening out
African girls. But one thing she could neither stand nor
understand about them was that 'they never told the truth'
and they were always giggling. They made her mad.

They say what broke her spirit was that one night, on
one of her regular nocturnal inspections, she found two girls
in bed together. Although the night was thick, they say they
saw that first she turned white. Then she turned red.

'Good Heavens, girl!

Is your mother bush?'
'No, Miss.'
'Is your father bush?'
'No Miss.'

'Then
Why
Are

You
Bush?'
Giggles, giggles, giggles.

Naughty African girls
Cracking up
To hear, and
See
European single woman
Tearing up herself over
Two girls in a bed.

But
Madam,
It is not
Just
Bush . . .
From knowledge gained since.

Hurrah for
The English wonder
The glorious
Understatement

Because
Madam,
It's not just b-u-s-h

But a
C-r-i-m-e
A Sin
S-o-d-o-m-y,

From knowledge gained since.
Sissie looked at the other woman and wished again that
at least, she was a boy. A man.
'So why are you crying?' she asked the other.
'It is nothing,' the other replied.

How then does one
Comfort her
Who weeps for
A collective loss?

They returned to the big kitchen. They must have done. And Marija must have laid the table for two. Brought out the cold cuts. Sliced cold ham. Sliced cold lamb. Pieces of cold chicken meat. Sliced cold sausages. Sliced cheese. Pickled olives. Pickled gherkins. Sauerkraut. Strange looking foods that tasted even stranger. Each of them stone cold. Yet all of them pulled out from the fridge or some corner of the kitchen with a loving familiarity.

Sissie would always puzzle over it. Cold food. Even after she had taught her tongue to accept them, she could never really understand why people ate cold food. To eat ordinary cooked food that has gone cold without bothering to heat it is unpleasant enough. But to actually chill food in order to eat it was totally beyond her understanding. In the end, she decided it had something to do with white skins, corn-silk hair and very cold weather.

Marija made coffee and then carried in the cake. Flat, fluffy and on top, the melting dark purple of jellied plums. Plums. It was altogether a feasty spread. Yet it was also clear that neither of them had a mouth for eating a plum cake. Or anything else for that matter. Breaking off little pieces after long intervals, putting them into their mouths, chewing, swallowing, chewing, swallowing.

Marija asked Sissie about her family.

'There are seven of us my mother's children and sixteen of us, my father's.' The two of them began to laugh. After the laughter, Sissie told Marija a little more about her family . . . about polygamy. What she always thought were some of its comforts, but admitting too that it was very unfair, basically.

When Sissie realised that the tension was broken, it occurred to her too that if Whoever created us gave us too much capacity for sorrow, He had, at the same time, built laughter into us to make life somewhat possible.

'When is your birthday?' Marija asked Sissie. The latter gave a reply.

They had been twins.
Their mother was three months pregnant

Before the great earthquake, and
They were ten months in the womb.

She too asked Marija's birth date. Just to be polite. Knowing she was going to forget that and many other things
besides. She who never remembered the day on which she
was born.

As usual, Marija took Sissie as far as the doorstep of the
youth hostel. Then suddenly, as they were saying good-
night, Sissie remembered that she would be leaving within
a week. In a few days she would be gone.

Goodbye to
One of the largest castles in all Germany
To silent pomp and decayed miseries.

Goodbye to Marija. She knew she could not tell Marija
about her imminent departure from the area. Not that
evening. No, it was not an evening to give undue intimations
of the passage of time, or of our mortality.

Seeing there are as many goodbyes as there are hellos,
and we die with each separation. Sissie knew she did not
possess the kind of courage it takes to have mentioned to
Marija at that time the fact that she was leaving the area
soon.

They split. When she entered her room, she discovered
that every one of her room-mates was asleep. It was just as
well, because neither she nor Marija had remembered the
customary brown paper bag and its fruity contents.

During the next few days, the campers stopped going to
the pine nursery. Instead, and as a rounding-off programme,
they were being taken round the Bavarian countryside,
seeing festivals and watching country dances. There was
always an air of gaiety wherever they went. And they drank
from famous shoe mugs, met country and district officials
who talked to them about educational reforms and their
country's contributions to international foreign aid to the
developing nations. And peace . . .

From knowledge gained since,
One wonders if their

Buxom wives had ever been
Guinea pigs to test
The pill and other
Drugs

As they say
Happens to
Miners' wives to
Farmers' wives in
Remote corners of
Banana republics and other
So-called-developing countries?

Oh.
Let me wail for
The Man we betrayed
The Man we killed

For,
Which other man lives
Here
Who dare tell
These guardians of my peace, and
Those
Exploiting do-gooders
To forget
My problems of

Ignorance
Disease
Poverty –

To stop
Their mediocre human loans

To stuff
Their pills where
They want them?

I know of
A mad geo-political professor
Whom no one listens to:

Who says
The danger has never been
Over-population.

For
The Earth has land to hold
More than twice the exploding millions
And enough to feed them too.

But
We would rather
Kill
            than
Think
        or
Feel.

My brother,
The new game is so
Efficient,
Less messy –

A few withered limbs
            just
A few withered seeds.

Ah-h-h
Lord,
Only a Black woman
Can
'Thank
A suicidal mankind'
With her
Death.

Her last evening came. Soon after Sissie and her companions
had returned from a trip to see the famous lakes and moun-
tains of the area, she was told that Marija was waiting at
reception for her. She changed quickly and went out to
meet her.

Marija could see that Sissie was tired. Maybe not too
tired to make talking to her unkind. But taking her through

the town, all the way to her house would have been too much. So they agreed they would only go for a walk around the castle and look at the river. Marija had brought Little Adolf with her and Sissie could feel some excitement in her. Already, uncertain of how to tell the other that this was indeed her last evening in the town, she waited for her to speak first.

'Tomorrow you come to eat lunch at my house, yes? I am going to cook. Big Adolf will be home.'

Sissie said quietly to Marija, 'I cannot come. I am sorry.'

The other stopped in her tracks immediately, her hands flying away from the handle of the pram. Her reaction startled the young child in the carriage and he started to cry. His mother picked him up and tried to comfort him. She had turned very pale. Then she turned very red. Sissie was almost delighted with this magic, this blushing and blanching. Meeting Marija was her first personal encounter with the phenomenon.

'Why you cannot come??'

At this point, Sissie began to feel ashamed and unhappy, for apart from everything else, she was afraid that in her agitation, Marija would drop her child.

'Why you cannot come?'

'I should have told you this before now. Long before now, Marija.'

'What it is?' asked Marija, as she returned her somewhat pacified child into the carriage. Obviously, mothers do not go dropping their offspring just-like-that.

'I am leaving tomorrow.'

'Ver you are going?'

'Back to the north.'

'Which norz?'

'Frankfurt, Hanover and Göttingen, where I shall be in another camp on the eastern border. Then after the camp, I shall leave for my country.'

'And you must go now, to this camp? From here, to-morrow?'

'Yes, Marija. I must show my face there at least for a few days.'

'This is weri sad, Sissie.'

So it was. The sadness was not in her words but in her voice. Her eyes. A sudden gust of air blew across from the river as though a ghost had passed. And whatever remained of the day folded itself up and died.

> Perhaps
> There are certain meetings
> Must not happen?
> Babies not born?
> Who come with nothing to enrich us,
> Too brief their time here –
>
> They leave us with
> Only
> The pains and aches for
> What-could-have-been-but-
> Was-not
>
> Wasted time and energies that
> Destroy our youth
> Make us older but
> Not wiser,
> Poorer for all that?

'And anyway, in a month's time, they will reopen my university.'

'One monz, Sissie: and you leave now here?'

They could not be rooted in one stop forever so without being aware of what they were doing, Marija started pushing her baby's carriage again, while Sissie kept pace with her.

Sissie was feeling absolutely cornered.

'You know, a month is not too much when you are travelling,' she said defensively.

'Ja-a-a?'

'I also have to make two other stops on the way.'

'Vai?'

'I have to visit some people.'

'Here? Germany?'

'One here. In Hamburg.'

'Vas to do in Hamburg? Who is there?'

'She is a friend. A girl . . .'

. . .

'When I was leaving my country, her mother made me promise that I shall not return home unless I go and see her daughter with my two eyes.'

'Vai?'

'So that I can tell her how she really is.'

'Ja?'

'Yes. You see, deep down, our people never feel good when their children come to Europe or go anywhere across the sea.'

'Vai?'

'Because anything can happen to them?'

'But people are in ze house. Something also happen there, Nein?'

'Marija, it is not easy to be reasonable every time.'

'Ja,' Marija agreed, subdued, perhaps with some awareness that she too is sometimes unreasonable? Then she said gingerly: 'Ze students, zey write letters home to their volks?'

'Yes,' Sissie agreed. 'But unless you are looking deep into the eyes of somebody how can you know he is telling the truth?'

'You cannot,' agreed the other woman.

'And if he is speaking from beyond the seas?'

'It is impossible, yes?'

'Yes, Marija. So our people have a proverb which says that he is a liar who tells you that his witness is in Europe.'

'Vitness? Vas is Vitness?'

'Like in court, someone to speak for your side.'

'Zat is a lawyer.'

'No. Not necessarily. I refer to just anybody who can claim he is in a position to know that the accused person did not say or do what he is accused of saying or doing.'

'Ja-ja. And your people, vas do zey say about a Vitness?'

'That any man who insists that his witness is in Europe is a liar.'

Marija giggled, betraying something of her former self.

'And vas in London you go to do?'

'I am meeting a boyfriend.'

She turned flaming red again.

'Ah zo. Ah zo. Ah zo. You are meeting a boyfriend. It is weri important, ja? And you must leave here weri quickly, ja?'

Sissie was feeling a little sick with Marija and her excitement over that piece of information. Of course, it would be rather nice to meet Whoever. But as for it being so important, she was not really sure. Could Marija be feeling jealous?

Marija said, 'Why you don't tell me before?'

'I forgot. I am sorry, Marija.'

'It is weri sad you forgot.'

> Why should we
> Always imagine
> Others to be
> Fools,
> Just because they love us?

Sissie felt like a bastard. Not a bitch. A bastard.

Marija said quivering, 'You know vas I have done, Sissie?'

'No, what have you done?'

'Ja. From ze butcher's I make order for a rabbit. Ze man brought it today. It is all fresh and clean. I cook specially for you. Tomorrow I cook . . . Big Adolf he will be home . . . Vee all eat together. You. Me. Little Adolf. Big Adolf.'

'O God, Marija, I cannot come. Listen, you know how they schedule a foreign visitor like me? They have sent all sorts of tickets, train, air, everything with definite boarding times booked.'

'. . .'

'Marija, there is nothing I can do about it. I suspect that even the campleader here . . .'

'But you did not tell me. And I said, Sunday I cook ze rabbit for Sissie.'

Suddenly, something exploded in Sissie like fire. She did not know exactly what it was. It was not painful. It did not hurt. On the contrary, it was a pleasurable heat. Because as she watched the other woman standing there, now biting her lips, now gripping at the handle of her baby's pram and looking so generally disorganised, she, Sissie wanted to laugh and laugh and laugh. Clearly, she was enjoying herself to see that woman hurt. It was nothing she had desired. Nor did it seem as if she could control it, this inhuman sweet sensation to see another human being squirming. It hit her like a stone, the knowledge that there is pleasure in hurting. A strong three-dimensional pleasure, an exclusive masculine delight that is exhilarating beyond all measure. And this too is God's gift to man? She wondered.

'Why didn't you let me know before you went to make all those elaborate plans?' Sissie demanded of the other woman.

'It was for you a surprise,' replied Marija timidly.

'Well, too bad. You'll have to eat my share of the rabbit for me.'

Marija's confusion knew no bounds.

Sissie could see it all. In her uncertain eyes, on her restless hands and on her lips, which she kept biting all the time.

But oh, her skin. It seemed as if according to the motion of her emotions Marija's skin kept switching on and switching off like a two-colour neon sign. So that watching her against the light of the dying summer sun, Sissie could not help thinking that it must be a pretty dangerous matter, being white. It made you awfully exposed, rendered you terribly vulnerable. Like being born without your skin or something. As though the Maker had fashioned the body of a human, stuffed it into a polythene bag instead of the regular protective covering, and turned it loose into the world.

Lord, she wondered, is that why, on the whole, they have had to be extra ferocious? Is it so they could feel safe here on the earth, under the sun, the moon and the stars?

Then she became aware of the fact that she would do something quite crazy if she continued on that trail of mind . . . Luckily for her, Marija was speaking anyway.

'I say . . . I say, Sissie, when you are leaving tomorrow?'

'. . . I am sorry, I didn't hear you the first time . . . some terrible hour in the morning. Very early.'

'Six o'clock and thirty minutes – yes? Zer is only one train zat goes from here to Munich early in ze morning.'

'Yes . . . yes. It must be that one.'

'I come see you off.'

"Why bother? There's no need to waste your morning sleep . . . I hate last minute goodbyes, anyway.'

Marija just stared at her. And she knew the last statement was totally unnecessary. There was a long pause during which neither said a thing. Then Marija resumed her pursuit.

'I vas going to cook in French sauce, the rabbit, mit vine und garlic und käse . . . cheese. Ja, Sissie?'

And Sissie noted for the first time that all along in the brief time of their friendship, obviously the worse Marija felt, the more Germanic was her English.

'You see, Marija,' said Sissie, trying not to let her irritation show, 'you said Big Adolf will be home tomorrow.'

'Ja.'

'Hm. You sure the rabbit was not for him?'

'But no . . . yes . . . but . . . but . . .'

'Well, pretend it was for him and cheer up . . . Besides, it is not sound for a woman to enjoy cooking for another woman. Not under any circumstances. It is not done. It is not possible. Special meals are for men. They are the only sex to whom the Maker gave a mouth with which to enjoy eating. And woman the eternal cook is never so pleased as seeing a man enjoying what she has cooked; eh, Marija? So give the rabbit to Big Adolf and watch him enjoy it. For my sake. And better still, for your sake.'

This time too Marija watched Sissie with a curious concentration. Yet she did not understand a word of it. Because serious as it sounded, Sissie was only telling a rather precious joke.

> After inflicting pain,
> We try to be funny
> And fall flat on our faces,
> Unaware that for
> The sufferer,

The Comedy is
The Tragedy and
That is the
Answer to the
Riddle.

They said goodbye and separated.

At the crack of dawn the following day, Sissie left the hostel with those few others from the group who also had to proceed to the north of the country.

Left one of the greatest castles of all
Germany . . .
Its river
Its dry moat
Its silent screams in dungeons
Gone into time –
Greedy warring owners
        and their
Whitened bones.

They only had a few minutes to wait before the train came. Then Sissie saw Marija running towards them clutching a brown paper bag. It occurred to her rather irrelevantly, that Marija had had to wake up quite early.

Marija crashed into Sissie, hugging her, smiling, and the one suspicious tear already glistening on the lashes of the left eye.

'O Marija,' Sissie said. And that was all she could say anyway. Then the train was there. They stood staring at one another, not finding words, which would have been meaningless anyhow.

Finally, Marija bent her head a little and kissed Sissie on the cheek. Our Sister did not encourage a feeling of outrage from herself, recognising in that gesture, a damned useful custom.

Meanwhile, her travel companions were beckoning Sissie to hurry up and board the train. Marija thrust the brown paper bag into her hands as she ran into the compartment. It was a local train and not crowded.

Sitting by the window, train whistling to warn of departure, Marija speaking hurriedly.

'Sissie, if you have time, in Munich, if your train have ze time, Sissie, before you go norz please don't miss it, stop in Munich, if only to spend a little time . . . please, Sissie, maybe for only two hours. Maybe zis morning. Zen you leave in ze afternoon. Yes?'

'Yes, Marija?'

'Because München, Sissie, is our city, Bavaria. Our own city . . . So beautiful you must see it, Sissie. I was going to take you zer. Ze two of us. To spend a day. Please, Sissie, see München. Zer is plenty music. Museums.'

The train moved. There on the platform stood Marija. To those for whom things were only what they seemed, a young Bavarian woman . . . not a teenager but not old either with dark brown hair cut short, very short, smiling, smiling, smiling, while one big tear trickled out of one of her eyes.

> München
> Marija
> Munich?
>
> No, Marija.
> She may promise
> But not fulfil –
>
> She shall not
> Waste a precious minute
> To see Munich and miss a train.
>
> Marija,
> There is nowhere in the
> Western world is a
> Must –
>
> No city is sacred,
> No spot is holy.
> Not Rome,
> Not Paris,
> Not London –

Nor Munich, Marija
And the whys and wherefores
Should be obvious.

Munich is just a place –
Another junction to meet a
Brother and compare notes.

She said, 'Hi Brother.'
He said, 'Hi Sister.'
'I am from Surinam.'
'I am from Ghana.'

They sat in a station restaurant
Ate with hefty German workers
Central European version of an
Afro-Spanish-Caribbean dish –
Chili-Corn-Carne
Dig?

And they talked of
Barcelona and bullfighting,
Spain –
Where an old man
Sits on a people's dreams –

Where they say there is no
Discrimination against BLACKS

Oh yeah?

When an empire decays,
Falls,
Its slaves are
Forgiven
Tolerated
Loved.
It might happen again, brother
It is happening now –
So let a Panther keep
Sharp
His claws and
His fangs . . .

Munich, Marija,
Is
The Original Adolf of the pub-brawls
and mobsters who were looking for
a
Führer –

Munich is
Prime Minister Chamberlain
Hurrying from his island home to
Appease,
While freshly-widowed
Yiddisher Mamas wondered
What Kosher pots and pans
Could be saved or not.

In 1965
Rhodesia declared herself independent
And the Prime Minister said, logically
From his island home –
'The situation remains
Unchanged,
We cannot fight
Our kith and kin.'

Or something to that effect.

Ach. München,
Marija,
Munich –
It is a pity, Marija,

But
Humans,
Not places,
Make memories.

Nein?

The train was determined to return Our Sister to her
origins. Soon the town disappeared from her sight. It was

too early for her to feel hungry, but out of curiosity, she opened up the brown bag. There were sandwiches of liver sausages, a few pastries, a slab of cheese, and some plums.

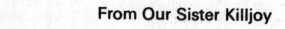

From Our Sister Killjoy

If anyone had told her that she would want to pass through England because it was her colonial home, she would have laughed.

She generally considered herself too smart to exhibit such weaknesses.

But to London she had gone anyway, consoling herself all the while that that was the only way to get people at home to understand where she had been. Abroad. Overseas.

Germany is overseas.

The United States is overseas.

But England is another thing.

What this other thing is, has never been clear to anyone.

France is surrounded by a special situational fog all her own. In the minds of the people at home, France exists, not as a separate country anywhere, but as reflected in her numerous colonial entities. For instance, all the relatives who had emigrated after the Second World War to the Ivory Coast to fish were talked of as having 'gone to French.'

They are a legend, those self-exiled Ghanaian fishing communities. They spread along the west coast of Africa, from the mouth of the Congo to the Gambia River. They could not have done better than the farmers they left at home.

Seeing that all that comes back are news of death, their own or of the children they bore.

She had had no idea of what to expect of England. But what no one had prepared her for, was finding so many Black people there.

Men, women, children.

The place seemed full of them but they appeared to be so wretched, she wondered why they stayed.

There were mothers pushing their babies in second-hand carriages while their men toiled the long day through as bus drivers, porters, construction workers, scavengers. Mostly scavengers.

Sissie bled as she tried to take the scene in.

The more people she talked to, the less she understood.

Two facts stood out though. Every man claimed that he

was a student, and so did every woman. The men were studying engineering or medicine or law.

But Sissie was not surprised to learn too that most of them had been students since the beginning of time.

The women were taking courses in dressmaking and hairdressing, they said.

Of course, there were the scholarship students, so-called because they were supported by either full or partial bursaries from the governments at home and who, for a time anyway, would therefore be conscious of the fact that if they did not finish up quickly and hurry back, their remittances would be cut off.

Then there were the recipients of the leftovers of imperial handouts:

> Post-graduate awards.
> Graduate awards.
> It doesn't matter
> What you call it.
>
> But did I hear you say
> Awards?
> Awards?
> Awards?
>
> What
> Dainty name to describe
> This
> Most merciless
> Most formalised
>
> Open,
> Thorough,
> Spy system of all time:
>
> For a few pennies now and a
> Doctoral degree later,
> Tell us about
> Your people
> Your history
> Your mind.

Your mind.
Your mind.

Tell us
Boy
How
We can make you
Weak
Weaker than you've already
Been.

And don't you get any ideas either
No
Radical
Interpretative
Nonsense from
You, Flatnose.

My brother,
There should be no misunderstanding,
No malice intended –

Indeed,
Our dear
Academic doctors
Deserve all
The worship
They get from our poor administrators at home
and more.

They work hard for the
Doctorates –
They work too hard,
Giving away
Not only themselves, but
All of us –

The price is high,
My brother,

Otherwise the story is as old as empires. Oppressed multitudes from the provinces rush to the imperial seat because
that is where they know all salvation comes from. But as

other imperial subjects in other times and other places have discovered, for the slave, there is nothing at the centre but worse slavery.

> Whether
> Warming itself up
> In a single cold room by a
> Paraffin lamp,
> Covering its
> Nakedness and
> Disappointed hopes with
> The old tickets of the
> Football pools
> or
> Glorious,
> With degrees.

Above all, what hurt our sister as she stood on the pavements of London and watched her people was how badly dressed they were. They were all poorly clothed.

The women especially were pitiful. She saw women who at home would have been dignified matrons as well as young, attractive girls looking ridiculous in a motley of fabrics and colours. Unused to the cold and thoroughly inefficient at dealing with it, they smothered their bodies in raiments of diverse lengths, hues and quality – in a desperate effort to keep warm:

> A blue scarf
> to cover the head and the ears,
> A brown coat lined with
> Cream synthetic fibre.
> Some frilly blouse,
> its original whiteness compromised.
> A red sweater
> with a button missing.
> An inch or two of black skirting
> showing under the coat.
> An umbrella,
> chequered green, rea and blue.

A pair of stockings that are too light for
A chocolate skin,
A pair of cheap shoes,
   Never-mind-what-colour,
But
Cheap.

The shoes. The shoes were always cheap. Cheap plastic versions of the latest middle-class fashions.

Sissie could console herself with only one thought. That against any other skin, such an assemblage of rags would have made the people look even more ridiculously pathetic than those Africans and West Indians actually did. But perhaps, this cold comfort was the gift of knowledge acquired later. For she knew from one quick composite vision, that in a cold land, poverty shows as nowhere else.

So as she rode the underground railway which the natives rightly call the Tube, and which, like all the other wonders, she was too busy with her own thoughts to appreciate, she became sad. So sad she wanted to cry. And sometimes she went to the little room she had taken for her short stay, and wept.

But that period lasted only a short time. Very soon, she started getting angry. Then she became very angry. At whatever drives our people to leave their warm homes to stay for long periods, and sometimes even permanently, in such chilly places. Winter in. Winter out.

Our poor sister. So fresh. So touchingly naive then. She was to come to understand that such migrations are part of the general illusion of how well an unfree population think they can do for themselves. Running very fast just to remain where they are.

She wondered why they never told the truth of their travels at home.

Not knowing that if they were to keep on being something in their own eyes, then they could not tell the truth to their own selves or to anyone else.

So when they eventually went back home as 'been-tos', the ghosts of the humans that they used to be, spoke of the wonders of being overseas, pretending their tongues craved for tasteless foods which they would have vomited to eat where they were prepared best.

Fish and Chips.

They lied.
They lied.
They lied.
The Been-tos lied.

And another generation got itself ready to rush out.

There was this bitterly cold night in London. She had crept very unwillingly out of her rather warm basement flat:

Rooms
Built out of a
Specially created
Hole in the ground
Under a house
For the sole occupation by
Human beings
Who do not have the
Wherewithal to acquire
Apartments
On and above ground level.

Sissie was meeting a friend who was arriving from West Africa, on some neo-colonial outfit that eventually proved the ruin of the very career it was supposed to advance for him. Not his fault. We all fall victim.

We have all fallen victim,
Sometime or
Other.

Always very considerate, the friend had written to ask her not to bother to go to either the airport or the terminal in town, but to meet him at his dingy but rather respectable penny-economy hotel. Which like dozens of its kind, was on the fringes of the West End, and where you could quite easily imagine that the junior officers from the outposts of the Empire stayed when they were on leave home, and where those day-and-night watchmen of the Empire probably stood and gazed at the real owners of the empire as they rode by, earlier on in coaches drawn by

> B-e-a-u-t-i-f-u-l-l-e-r groomed
> Horses,
> And later,
> In Daimlers and Royces . . .
>
> Most of them had
> Scottish names
> Or Irish
> Or Welsh.
> The day-and-night watchmen, that is.
>
> There
> Must be a
> Mensah in every town,
> Every region its
> Sambo.
>
> So they did make sense after all.
> The grey
> Menopausing
> Lady-on-the-bus and
> The pink
> Bright-eyed
> Welsh
> Cockney
> Lass-on-the-train.

One had said, 'You say you come from Ghaanna? Then we have a lot in common!' Sissie didn't know what to do with the statement, uncertain of whether it was a threat or a promise.

'We had chiefs like you,' the Scot went on, 'who fought one another and all, while the Invader marched in.' Sissie thanked her, but also felt strongly that their kinship had better end right there.

Livingstone the Saint
Opening
Africa up for
Rape.
Scottish missions everywhere
In Tumu-Tumu and Mampong –
They did love the familiar
                mountain air, those
Hardy Highlanders!

'Yes,' screamed the Scot and
'No,' she screamed.
'Why should you judge
Scotland
By her traitors?
Ach, what waste our men and brains!
What could
England have done without ·
Scottish shipping too?
Fleming
Discovering
Penicillin
For
England to
Glory in?'

She politely telling her
She couldn't really judge,
Seeing
Her cute degree in English Hons.,
Was gotten
From
Burns
Bruce
    and
McPherson.

As for the Welsh maid from East Putney, she spoke for a
good hour and more, about a farewelling, somewhere in
London Town.

'It's a paa-r-rty, y'see, for one of our boys. He's given up
everything to go 'ome and 'elp organise . . .'

> And all the time, she spoke
> With such earnestness,
> Such confidential whisper
> And frightening intensity,
> She could have passed for a soul sister,
> But for her colour
>   – and our history.

But then, it is also quite obvious that the world is not filled
with folks who shared our sister's black-eyed squint at things.
It is not at all likely. And if there are one or two who do,
they certainly do not include the German-born American
Professor in the Humanities who zoomed into her house
one afternoon, panting, sweating and literally foaming at the
mouth, and claiming he had come from the United States
and would go back two whole journeys across the Atlantic,
just to convince her of one thing. That this thing binds the
Germans, the Irish and the Africans – in that order naturally
– together. And that this thing is, OPPRESSION.

'Ja, our people have been oppressed for many many
years, since the First World War,' he said. Our Sister's own
mouth caught so rigidly open with surprise, and wide
enough for a million flies to swarm in and out, how could she
ask him:

> 'Germans?
> Oppressed?
> By whom?'

Yes, so frozen was her mind with the icy brilliance of this
master discovery, she could not ask him whether after the
Germans, the Irish and Africans – indisputably in that
order – there are or could have been some other oppressed
peoples on the earth, like Afro-Americans or Amerindians
or Jews.

> She forgot to ask
> Her Most Learned Guest

    If he had heard of
    Buchenwald,
                or come across
    Dachau
                even in his reading?

She was remembering a younger German, just the summer
before, inquiring most politely, if in Africa, they think
Germans are racists.

'No,' Sissie had answered quite frankly, 'where I come
from, we only think of you as makers of the Volkswagen, the
Mercedes-Benz and supposedly reliable brands of other
goodies in science and technology.' The young man had
smiled and looked very grateful.

Sissie was thinking too, as she sat facing her German-
born American professor in the Humanities, that we are a
joke. Us over here. And she was fully aware too that that is
already too sick a cliché to laugh at. Because it is really true
that we are all a joke, both the pigs who run our countries
and us the chickens who criticise them. For she was trying to
figure out what could happen when that professor in the
Humanities and genius in both Forgetfulness and Invention
presented an economic corollary of his brand of history to
an influential African.

                Who no sabe book
                Sabe notin' for e contrey
                no fit hear notin' self.

Oga, 'this big Africa man go sit down te-e-ey, look at this
Onyibo man wey e talk, wey e mout- go ya, ya, ya,' then your
African would obsequiously get up, and with due apology
offer the other gentleman something like the world's most
expensive liquor, then gingerly sit down again in his own
armchair imported from either Sweden or Italy, and
sweating and stammering, offer something else to the other
gentleman, but this time his mother for sale at a take-away
price, which he is still prepared to reconsider, and with himself, his brothers and sisters, wife and children all thrown in
as bonus . . .

94

                              beautiful,
                              no?

Especially when you think this is what has been happening
anyway, every minute, every day, since Ghana opened a
dance of the masquerades called Independence, for Africa.

And so there was Sissie, all bundled up, on her way to
meet a friend. She discovered on arrival that he was already
at the hotel, and someone else was with him. A relative,
whose name was Kunle, practically a Londoner, having
lived in that city for seven years.

As it turned out, uppermost in all their minds, was not the
war in Nigeria.

                         We are used to
                         Tragedy, you know,
                         The scale hardly makes a difference –

but the transplant. The Heart Transplant. The evening
papers had screeched the news in with the evening trains
of the Underground. Of how the Dying White Man had
received the heart of a coloured man who had collapsed on
the beach and how the young coloured man had allegedly
failed to respond to any efforts at resuscitation and therefore
his heart had been removed from his chest, the Dying White
Man's own old heart having been cleaned out of his chest
and how in the meantime the Dying White Man was doing
well, blah, blah, blah!

                         It is funny. But among a
                         Certain rural Fantis,
                         It is believed that cutting the throat
                         Of a pig is simply
                         Useless: the
                         Only way to get your good pork
                         Is to tear the heart out of the chest of a
                         Squealing pig – the louder he
                         Squeals, the better the pork.

The Christian Doctor's Second Triumph.
    She was to remember her friend's relation proclaiming it

the most wonderful piece of news to have come his way in
a very long time . . .

> Confused, yet dying to ask Kunle
> Why?
> How?
>
> Admonishing herself to tread
> Softly –
> We are in the region of
> SCIENCE!
>
> Little
> Village
> Girls
>   who
> Dream
> Do not
> Cannot
> Ever
> Understand
> These things
> – it matters not what else they claim –
>
> Besides, the pathways of
> History
> Are littered with the bones of
> Those who dared doubt
> Progress and . . .

But really, Sissie could have spared herself the guilt of anti-
science self-accusations. Kunle was on a more interesting,
more practical wavelength. When both Sissie and her friend
managed to ask why he felt the way he did about the heart
transplantation, Kunle answered them most eagerly:

> that he was sure it is the
> type of development that can
> solve the question of apartheid
> and rid us, 'African negroes
> and all other negroes' of the
> Colour Problem. The whole of the
> Colour Problem.

At one point, they also asked him if he had ever thought of whose hearts, donor and receiver, might have been used in the earlier stages of what they were sure could only have been a fairly long series of trials that had exploded into those headlines.

> That was some years
> Before
> A colleague described
> The Christian Doctor's nth triumph as being
>   'Dangerously close to outright
>   experimentation.'
> Poor anonymous colleague
> Jealous, possibly, of the
> 'Sudden Fame' of the
> 'Scientific Luminary'
> 'Jet-set Celebrity', his
> Tempestuous Romances and his
> Constantly nourished
> Constantly pampered
> Image '

'O yes' answered Kunle eagerly, 'he must have experimented on the hearts of dogs and cats.'

As for Sissie, she lost speech.

But her friend still had his voice, bless his composure.

So he screamed at Kunle, 'You mean you believe it was dogs' and cats' hearts all the way until the first recipient of a living heart from that woman?'

> He meant that first
> Announced
> Donor – poor ghostly female whose
> Identity has
> Faded,
> Already,
> So completely.

What were they trying to get at, wondered Kunle very angrily. He then proceeded to explain patiently to them that the Christian Doctor is a Scientist, and that if he had ever tried on a single human heart before . . .

> Too scared to stop the flow and
> Whisper,
> 'There always must be
> Two hearts, you know,
> Not one.'

He would have announced it to the world either as soon as it had happened or at least, later in any of the numerous interviews he had given following the first transplantation. This time, even the friend could not say a word. But Sissie found herself giggling. Then she laughed openly with relief, declaring to herself,

> Dear Lord,
> I believe
> Only in the
> Survival of
> My kind:
>
> I have to –
> I have to –
>
> And if a
> Great Scientist comes out
> One fine Cape morning with a
> Successful transplant of
> Two human hearts,
> Saying he
> Experimented only on
> Dog hearts or
> Cat hearts –
>   Lord
> I shall not
> Question his
> Morality,
>   Seeing
> I am not of
> The society for

The prevention of cruelty to man's
Dumb friends or any
Selfless group.

But perhaps,
It is with dog hearts
As with man's?
Burning with indigestion
Bobbing up and
Bobbing down with
Love
   and
Grief?
Forgive me
Kunle and other good men –

I know
Dogs
   and
Cats are
Such
Darling Cutie Creatures,
But . . .

My dear brother,

I have been to a cold strange land where dogs and cats
eat better than many many children;

Where men would sit at table and eat with animals, and
yet would rather die then shake the hands of other men.

Where women who say they have no time to bear children
and spoil their lives would sit for many hours and feed baby
dogs delicate food with spoons, and make coats to cover the
hairy animals from the same cloth they wear, as sisters and
brothers and friends in our village would do on festive
occasions.

My brother, I have been to a land where they treat
animals like human beings and some human beings like
animals because they are not
               Dumb enough.

Sissie had wanted to tell Kunle that our hearts and other parts are more suitable for surgical experiments in aid of the Man's health and longevity. Because although we are further from human beings than dogs or cats, by some dictate of the ever-capricious Mother Nature, our innards are more like the Man's than dogs' or cats' . . .

> Of course, it is not easy to follow.
> But then, to live in peace in Man's world
> The Virgin Birth
> Is not the only mystery
> One
> Simply
> Has to take
> By faith.

And anyway, the Christian Doctor has himself said that in his glorious country, niggerhearts are so easy to come by, because of the violence those happy and contented bantus perpetrate against one another, in their drunken ecstasies and childlike gambols.

> After all, every
> Well-informed,
> Reasonable,
> Individual
> Knows:
> That those
> Other blacks are
> More urbanised and
> Command a
> Better standard of living
> Than
> Any other Africans
> Anywhere on the continent.
> You simply cannot compare.
> O-o-ow,
> Those bantus
> Are being
> S-o-o-o well-looked-after

> The others?
> It's a laugh!
> Look at the mess they've made of
> Independence given them.

Kunle was obviously in touch with reasonable well-informed circles. And just an attempt on Sissie's part to open her mouth to contradict anything he had to say got him mad.

> Yet she had to confess she still had not
> managed to come round to seeing Kunle's point:
> that cleaning the Baas's chest of its rotten
> heart and plugging in a brand-new, palpitatingly
> warm kaffirheart, is the surest way to usher in
> the Kaffirmillennium.

Disgraceful imbecility. Her half normal self regretted her inability to share Kunle's vision even then. His eyes shone and his whole body trembled with the ecstasy of it.

> Already
> Many years ago
> Each year
> Retreating with a
> Louder laugh
> Than the One-That-Went-Before.
> Dying White Man
> is
> Dead.
> THE DONOR'S heart
> Lived for a year and more,
>   we heard, while
> His name
> Lived an evening's news.
> Wife of Dying-White-Man-Now Dead
> Should have made a little
> Money from
> His insurance policy against
> Surgical risks, and all the nice
> TV coverage of him
> Cheering a
> Horse to

Victory,
But
His daughter says her
Mother has got
No
Money, her
Daddy suffered terribly,
And
She herself is
Confused.

Meanwhile
One or two more
Idealistic
Young
Refugees
Have gone totally
Mad – or got themselves killed on
The Zambezi.
The Christian Doctor has
Taken a couple of press pictures
In the company of a
Movie Queen

Divorced
Mrs Christian Doctor

Acquired another
Mrs Christian Doctor
and a couple of rand
Millions
Effected quite a few more
Heart transplantations.
He is the only one
Who seems
Now to be doing well;
The rest?
A veritable catalogue of
Death and just plain
Heartbreak.

As for
Dying White Man's daughter's
Black neighbours,
Only a few more
Millions
Have had to carry passes, to
Breathe
Where they
Work,
Just a coupla thousands
Raided and
Arrested,
A few dead from torture
Just a few more hanged . . .
Pain and decay
Are certainties
Are endless:
De Gaulle has died
   and
By his graveside,
An African Head of State has
Cried;

They say
He shed
Real tears, for
De Gaulle and France:
His two loves and,
Lovers,
Who send
Guns
Planes and
Submarines to Vorster, for the
Protection of Africa.

'My friend Edward Health'
said Dr. Bushia one day in 1971.

KUNLE has died,
Killed by the car for which he had
Waited so long:

Frozen fingers in winter,
Cheap nigger-food from Shepherds Bush
Hot faces in hiding from
Sneering mouths that wonder
When
You are going to
Finish, and go back home . . .

And the letters from home,
My god,
THOSE LETTERS FROM HOME!
Letters
For which we died expecting and
Which
Buried us when they came . . .

'Kofi,
when are you coming?
there is nothing bad here
we are well and we are hoping you are
well too and we pray The Almighty in
His Goodness shall protect you.'

'Bragou,
There is nothing bad here
. . . except our family is
drowning in debts.
even the things which were always good
have gone wrong with us this year.'

'Dede,
we did not finish dividing
the expenses from your grandmother's funeral and libation
observances before your small aunt whose husband had
refused to give her a plot to cultivate at the beginning of the
year's planting was discovered with The Big Cough. We
hear there is a cure for it these days. But it is not easy for
people like us to hear of such things and we do not know
where to go and find it.'

'. . . Obi,
please keep this to yourself
and bear it like a man.
And maybe it is not true,
but I hear they shelled
your father's compound in the night,
the whole place went up in flames
there were no survivors . . .'

But
please
Kunle,
if only you were here.
Now
it is me,
Your Own Mother
speaking.

There is nothing bad here

And I am not complaining
My Child.
You also know
we are proud
that
you are Overseas.

But when I see some women are getting well-looked after by
their children who only finished low-low schooling, I think
hard. Every day I tell myself I must have patience and that
no one ever got full reward for doing half-job.

But this year, Kunle, it is like when all the houses here
swept out the evils from their courtyards, they threw them
into our own. Your small small sister the sixth-born, who was
only walking by the teacher's leg when you were leaving . . .
ah, how the teacher said she did well in her learning? But
Kunle, she had her first menstruation this rainy season past.
And already she has been impregnated!! The boy, God
himself is looking and listening if I lie: Kunle, the boy who
impregnated your sister is a no-good loafer who finished
school two years ago and does not want to work even to

feed his own self. I have cried many nights over this business. And the twins passed the test to go to College but there was no money and you were not here. And apart from you, who else do we have? The girl was going to be lucky because you will be here when it is time for her to go to College. But now look at what has happened.

Kunle,
I am not complaining
Because I know God sends

us trouble only to test us. Though for one trouble we have just got, I do not know. Do you remember those people of That House who have many people and much money? They always envied us our little land. And now the head of their house who is only as old as your own small self? He has been doing well and we hear he is in with the new people of the Government. So now all the big people of the Government in this district are behind this boy helping him to take our land. Our very small land. We even borrowed some money which is too big to mention to give to some important men who told us they could help us. They have also eaten our money and now it is very clear that they are on the side of the others.

Kunle,
I am not begging
you for
money.
Am I not a mother?
Do I not know you need

money yourself, and if I was rich like my friends, would I not send you some myself?

But my son,
there is
nothing here at all. So if someone gives you a penny gift, send half to us.

Finally,
may God protect you where you are and bring you back soon. For there are many jobs waiting for you to do . . .'

> The jobs were waiting
> Properly waiting,
> And there were many.

So many in fact that Kunle, like so many of us, wished he had had the courage to be a coward enough to stay forever in England. Though life 'home' has its compensations. The aura of having been overseas at all. Belonging to the elite, whatever that is. The sweet pain of getting a fairly big income which can never half support one's own style of living, not to mention the inescapable responsibilities.

> And there had to be a
> Car –
> Plain Transportation Necessity
> With just a little
> Prestige on the side.

Anybody who had known him in London could testify that he was a first class driver. But then what is the point in owning a special car in Africa if you are going to drive yourself to your village? So it is quite likely that Kunle's chauffeur did not have half his master's steering experience.

. . . The car itself had burnt to its original skeleton, its passengers to ashes, with Kunle trapped between the door on his side and a tyre, screaming, screaming unheard, his heart vigorous, long after his voice had gone.

> Yes,
> Kunle's heart stayed in
> His chest, too strong to be
> Affected by anything else,
> Still pumping under the
> Sizzling chest,
> Stopping only when
> The flames had
> Swallowed it up.
> Poor Kunle
> Poor Christian Doctor.
> What waste
> What utter waste.

For it certainly would have gladdened Kunle's heart to find itself in the hands of the Christian Doctor.

> A thoroughly civilised
> Meeting.
>
> But it is a long way from
> Lagos-and-Ibadan, to
> A White Southern hospital.
> And anyway –
> Wherever they are and from whatever causes,
> My God,
> Black people still
> Die
> So
> Uselessly!

. . . for although the policy had been absolutely comprehensive, the insurance people had insisted it did not cover a chauffeur driving át 80 m.p.h. on the high road. That is deliberately courting trouble, you kn-a-a-uw. And like all of us who have been to foreign places, Kunle could recognise quality service when he saw it. He had taken out his policy with a very reliable insurance company . . . Foreign, British, terribly old and solid, with the original branch in London and cousins in Ottawa, Sydney, Salisbury and Johannesburg . . .

A Love Letter

Said an anxious Afro-American student to a visiting African professor, 'Sir, please, tell me: is Egypt in Africa?'

'Certainly,' replied the professor.

'I mean Sir, I don't mean to kind of harass you or anything,' pressed the student, 'but did the Egyptians who built the pyramids, you know, the Pharaohs and all, were they African?'

'My dear young man,' said the visiting professor, 'to give you the decent answer your anxiety demands, I would have to tell you a detailed history of the African continent. And to do that, I shall have to speak every day, twenty-four hours a day, for at least three thousand years. And I don't mean to be rude to you or anything, but who has that kind of time?'

My Precious Something,
            First of all, there is this language. This
language.

Yes, I remember promising you that I was going to try
and be positive about everything. Since you reminded me
that the negative is so corrosive. You even went on to give
me an illustration of what you meant with an example from
Medicine. That negativism is malign, like cancer. It chokes
all life within its reach as it grows . . .

I nodded agreement, my eyes lighting up at how pro-
fessionally clear you always are. But I remember too that
when I attempted to grasp your point better by suggesting
a political parallel, that negativism then must be like the
expansion of western civilisation in modern times, because
it chokes all life and even eliminates whole races of people
in its path of growth, you said, laughing:

'There you go again, Sissie, you are so serious.'

But how can I help being serious? Eh, My Love, what
positive is there to be, when I cannot give voice to my soul
and still have her heard? Since so far, I have only been able
to use a language that enslaved me, and therefore, the
messengers of my mind always come shackled?

I know you would scream at me, full of laughter, pacing
the tiny room, your quick steps eating up its spaces every
now and then:

'Shackled? Sissie, your thoughts? Don't you think you
are overdoing the modesty bit? Maybe you would feel
embarrassed if you tried to be lyrical about the freshness of

the air at mid-winter or the essence of polite conversation for those who go to tea with the English royal family. But your thoughts on any other subject never come shackled.... Someone else's perhaps. But yours? No. And you know it, Sissie.'

I would feel a warmness creeping around my neck at your appreciation of me. Yet I would also be aware of a certain anxiety. To press my point. That I meant it symbolically, referring to many areas of our lives where we are unable to operate meaningfully because of what we have gone through. By now you would be losing your patience. I know you would. In fact, I can hear your response, coming clearly.

'Dear Lord, all you radicals make me sick. How oversensitive do you people want to be? What exactly do you mean by "many areas of our lives where we are unable to operate meaningfully?" Listen, why do you people like to imprison time? Eh? Hei, don't freeze time. Don't lock it up in a capsule of tragic visions. Let it be, so that it can move. Let time move.'

Your eyes would get quite fierce and I would feel ashamed.

But I know that I am also right. Of course, I agree with you about letting time move. But, My Darling, we have got to give it something to carry. Time by itself means nothing, no matter how fast it moves. Unless we give it something to carry for us; something we value. Because it is such a precious vehicle, is time.

But it is at such points that you storm out of the room with me wondering whether I should not call you back to let you know that in spite of insisting on holding my ground during these futile arguments, I still love you, whatever that means.

Of course, the language of love does not have to be audible. It is beyond Akan or Ewe, English or French. Therefore if I was not articulate enough in that area, then the fault must lie somewhere else.

But there are some matters which must be discussed with words. Definitely. At least, by those of us who by the grace of God still have our tongues in our mouths. May Allah be praised.

And it is here that I wail and scream. When I think of the position I find us in. Because although I keep reminding myself that I love you – whatever that means – we were never able to discuss some of these matters relating to our group survival. No, never without it ending in one of us getting angry and the other feeling hurt.

Why? It's because we do not share a private world. You are always doing your best to convince me that human beings are human beings.

Of course, My Dear, but don't you think it is almost impossible to believe in all that considering some of the things we have learnt?

For instance, it is quite clear now that all of the peoples of the earth have not always wished one another well. Indeed we are certain now, are we not, that so many people have wished us ill. They wish us ill. They have always done. They still do.

And now we know why. It is such an old story. Such a painful one too. Otherwise, how could they have made slaves of us when we owed them nothing? Not a cent, not a pesewa, not a kobo. Oh, it is not easy to understand. To think that we owed nobody the smallest franc. Yet they wanted our labour for free. And when with the help of the gun and some of our own relatives they succeeded in sitting on us, they then said that indeed, we were made to be slaves because we are stronger, and we can work longer hours in the sun, and such other nonsenses . . .

My question is: who was there when we were saying farewell to our God? My Darling, we are not responsible for anybody else but ourselves. We did not create other races. So we should not let others make us suffer because we are stronger than them or have better skins.

Sickle cell anaemia. High blood pressure. Faster heartbeats in infancy. One truth maybe. A whole lot of wishful thinking. No amount of pseudo-scientific junk is going to make us a weaker race than we are. And may they come to no good who wish us ill. After all, what baby doesn't know that the glistening blackest coal also gives the hottest and the most sustained heat? Energy. Motion. We are all that.

Yes, why not? . . . A curse on those who for money would ruin the Earth and trade in human miseries.

We have always produced great minds. But good God, I refuse to think that the man from the icy caves of the north could have been one of our inventions. Yet sometimes one wonders, considering the ferocity with which he has been attacking us. As though we were to blame for his feelings of inadequacy. Both physical and otherwise. Especially physical.

It all sounds like science fiction. Like the story of Frankenstein. But then, science fiction is only a wild extension of reality, no?

My Love, perhaps some people are hiding some very frightening collective secrets. And if they are, then human beings are not just human beings. Since there can be no total mutual understanding where there is no total candour, Unasikia, Mpenzi Wangu?

So you see, My Precious Something, all that I was saying about language is that I wish you and I could share our hopes, our fears and our fantasies, without feeling inhibited because we suspect that someone is listening. As it is, we cannot write to one another, or speak across the talking cables or converse as we travel on a bus or train or anywhere, but we are sure they are listening, listening, listening.

You already know how unhappy the situation makes me, anyway.

Naturally, with your supreme sense of the practical, you have tried to make me see the situation in another way. That the fact that you and I can meet and talk at all is an advantage to the present. Yes, indeed. Except that if the old people are right, that whatever is sweet has some bitterness in it, then we have to determine the amount of bitterness we take from the sweetness of the present. Otherwise, there'll be so much bitterness, we shall never know there was anything else around.

Besides, in the old days, who knows, we could have been born in the same part of the land. Or we could have met when they brought me as a novice to understudy one of the famous priestesses in your area or when they sent you to be apprenticed to one of our goldsmiths. Maybe, it's all nostalgia and sentimental nonsense. Again, why not? Why should I be afraid of being sentimental? In any case, the question is not just the past or the present, but which factors out of both the past and the present represent for us the most dynamic forces for the future.

That is why, above all, we have to have our secret language. We must create this language. It is high time we did. We are too old a people not to. We can. We must. So that we shall make love with words and not fear of being overheard.

As for some other people watching and listening to us, u-huh. They pretend they are not interested in our carryings-on. But really, you would think that is all they do. Sometimes, you feel their eyes beaming so high behind you, you fear they are almost drilling holes into the skin on your back. Trying to find out how we dance, how we make love, how we reason.

Of course, we are different. No, we are not better than anybody else. But somewhere down the years, we let the more relaxed part of us get too strong. So that the question was never that of changing into something that we have never been. No, we only need to make a small effort to update the stronger, the harder, the more insensitive part of ourselves. Like catching up with modern versions of ancient cruelties!

Burning people's farms, poisoning their rivers and killing all their trees and plants as part of the effort to save them from a wicked philosophy.

Supplying brothers with machine guns and other heavy arms because you want to stop them from slaughtering one another.

Making dangerous weapons that can destroy all of the earth in one little minute, in order to maintain peace.

My Dear, there seem to be so many things I would like to tell you – see what I mean about language?

When I started to write this letter, I thought I just wanted to say how much I have missed you. How much I still miss you. I know you will not believe it. Besides, what difference will it make even if you believed me? . . . But your image is before me all the time. Like the spirit of someone I have wronged. And yet I have not wronged you, have I? Indeed, if there is anyone I may have sinned against, it is me. That desiring you as I do, needing you as I do, I still let you go. I should have been more careful, really. In fact, all sorts of well-wishers have told me what I should have done in the first place, loving you as much as I claim to, whatever that means. They say that any female in my position would have thrown away everything to be with you, and remain with you: first her opinions, and then her own plans. But oh deliciously naive me. What did I rather do but daily and loudly criticise you and your friends for wanting to stay forever in alien places?

Maybe I regret that I could not shut up and meekly look up to you even when I knew I disagreed with you. But you see, no one had taught me such meekness. And I wish they had.

Sometimes when they are hotly debating the virtues of the African female, I ask myself: 'But who am I? Where did I come from?'

My Precious, as I told you some time ago, when I was chatting to you about my background, the village is over two hundred and fifty miles from the coast. Both my mother and father had not been to school at all. So no one could accuse them of having got acculturated. They definitely had not been overseas and therefore were not westernised. And since none of them had ever lived anywhere near a modern town, they could not possibly be urbanised. Given all of that, if they didn't know how I should have been brought up as an African woman, then who does?

No, My Darling: it seems as if so much of the softness and meekness you and all the brothers expect of me and all the sisters is that which is really western. Some kind of hashed-up Victorian notions, hm? Allah, me and my big mouth!!

See, at home the woman knew her position and all that. Of course, this has been true of the woman everywhere – most of the time. But wasn't her position among our people a little more complicated than that of the dolls the colonisers brought along with them who fainted at the sight of their own bleeding fingers and carried smelling salts around, all the time, to meet just such emergencies as bleeding fingers?

There I go again. But please, Dear Heart, I only wished to say that we have been caught at the confluence of history and that has made ignorant victims of some of us, it seems. Because if what I felt and still feel for you is any indication, then I should have taken you. And too bad that I didn't know how. Now it is quite clear even to me that having political quarrels with a man or insisting that once he has finished his studies abroad he should go home, are not any of the more recognised ways to enchant him. In fact, any form of argument is bad, period. Yet, all these are 'facts' I am just learning. How far can one really be blamed for being born naïve, eh? Or for not catching the survival lines in a terribly confused social stream?

This is the other problem. Me always blaming myself even when there is nothing the matter with anything. Of course, there is something the matter with everything. Great cataclysmic faults of the ages. An enemy has thrown a huge boulder across our path. We have been scattered. We wander too far. We are in danger of getting completely lost. We must not allow this to happen.

You are saying, 'There goes Sissie again. Forever carrying Africa's problems on her shoulders as though they have paid her to do it.' I am ashamed of these preoccupations. Because you were always trying to get me to realise that the faults indeed are too old and they have sunk too deep into the fabric of our lives to be corrected in a day. That is, even if we were to start doing something about them immediately. Unfortunately, it doesn't look like we are ready or anxious to.

But My Beloved, I could not believe that you had left finally. That you did not intend to come back. For days, I kept hoping that I would hear a knock on the door, open it and find you standing there with the black airline bag slung on your shoulder and a lot of unspoken mischief shining through your eyes. Just like you used to do. But you never came back.

It did hit me eventually, but it was after some time though. And then I did not know what to do with myself. It was like a possession. Of course, as everyone would just love to re-mind me, if I had any womanliness in me, it should have come out then.

'You know where he lived, didn't you? You should have just gone there and told him you are sorry, never mind what for. Cream up to him . . . If you love your man, take him, by any means necessary.'

It may sound impossibly droll to other people but as I keep saying, none of all this occurred to me. I just sat in my room and suffered. I didn't go mad as I feared, Allah is truly great. Something else happened though. Loneliness became my room-mate and took the place over.

My Dear, I was lonely before, when I was home.

I shall be lonely again. O yes, everyone gets lonely some time or other. After all, if we look closer into ourselves, shall we not admit that the warmth from other people comes so sweet to us when it comes, because, we always carry with us the knowledge of the cold loneliness of death?

So please do not say that what I felt after you left was part of my . . . How did you describe it? 'Anti-western neurosis?' Maybe. Though I confess too that I am convinced these cold countries are no places for anyone to be by themselves. Man, chicken, or goat. There is a kind of loneliness overseas which is truly bad. It comes with the cold wind blowing outside the window making the trees moan so. It is there in the artificial heat in the room which dried my skin and filled my sleep with nightmares.

It comes with the food from the store. The vegetables and the fruits that never ever get rotten. The meat, the chicken. All of which have been filled with water so that they will look bigger and give the sellers more money.

My Lost Heart, loneliness pursued me there in the unwholesome medications on the food that I had to eat out of tins, boxes and plastic bags, just a taste of which got my blood protesting loudly through the rashes and hives it threw on my body. Now my skin, which you used to say was so soft and smooth is gone hard and rough like the shell of an aged tortoise.

Forgive me, My Darling, that my fears should be often so insane. You, with your ecumenical sympathies have always tried to get me to realise that whatever other people eat and live on is good for all human beings. And the Elders in their infinite wisdom, declared a long time ago that the unsavoury innards of the possum may be a delicacy for somebody else somewhere. Okay, okay, okay. All I wanted to say is that sometimes, I missed plain palm-oil on boiled greens.

That is why it should not have come as a surprise to you that I spent many sleepless nights trying to understand why, after finishing their studies, our brothers and sisters stay here and stay and stay.

After all, was it not part of the original idea that we should come to these alien places, study what we can of what they know and then go back home?

As it has turned out, we come and clearly learn how to die. Yes, that must be it. And it is quite weird. To come all this way just to learn how to die from a people whose own survival instincts have not failed them once yet. Not once. Forgive me for being so morbid. I can't help it. You once said that I do not laugh enough. That I must try to laugh more. You are right, of course. And I remember how my old friends and I used to scream with mirth at home, looking at how we were all busy making fools of ourselves. Especially the men in high places. Oh, we laughed until our sides ached, then collapsed on the floor and groaned at the sheer madness of it all, while tears streamed down our cheeks. Maybe it was the sun and the ordinary pleasure of standing on our own soil . . . Our beautiful land. Did I say our land? One wonders whether it is still ours. And how much longer it will continue to be . . .

A curse on all those who steal continents! . . .

My Beloved, looking at and listening to the perfected versions of our loss of perspective here would wipe the bravest grin from anyone's face. We have become past masters at fishing out death, no matter what package it comes in. Just like the big-time professors at home. Who, knowing what a back-breaking job it is to unlearn what the masters have taught, and that to learn anything new is even more difficult, spend the little time between beers, advising us against 'putting back the clock, reversing history', wioh, wioh,

wioh!! They say that after all, literature, art, culture, all information, is universal. So we must hurry to lose our identity quickly in order to join the great family of man . . .

My Dear, isn't that truly crazy? How can they say these things? . . . Oh yes, I remember once when I was going on furiously about these comatose intellectuals, you told me to save my breath 'because they are gone, gone, gone.' Looking at your beautiful hand – it was the left – waving in the air and your great eyes rolling in their sockets, I couldn't help giggling. And I remembered the auctioneers at church 'harvests' with their little bells. Yes, My Love, they are indeed gone, gone, gone.

Yet, My Sweetheart, the tale is not done being told. For this self-exile seems to be only a younger version of the old bankruptcy. Do you remember the first time we met? At the students' union meeting? And I got up to attack everybody, pleading that instead of forever gathering together and virtuously spouting such beautiful radical analyses of the situation at home, we should simply hurry back? I haven't forgotten how ridiculous I felt at first, with my righteous anger. They nearly ate me up, you remember? When the meeting was formally over, they all rushed on me, yelling at me, pounding me with their arguments. Then I didn't feel ridiculous any more, only sad. For that is also the tragedy – trying to explain their decisions not to go home. So many versions and each new one more pathetic and less convincing than the one before.

'Sissie, you know how it is at home. People are fascinated by titles. So that although I don't care to be called Dr. Anything, you still have to admit they only begin to treat you like a human being when you have a Ph.D.'

That got me. I fumbled, looking for something to say. And yet what could I say to that? When men who themselves barely made their first degrees now insist on employing only those with three degrees or more? Blessed are those who got to the market-place first: they shall scramble for the best.

Meanwhile, the thesis is forever getting written. And for years we subconsciously ward off its conclusions. Since completing it only deprives us of one good excuse for continuing to stay here. But it is only one of the excuses though.

'Sissie, you don't know, some of us have tried really hard to go back. I for instance wrote to the bank. I wrote to the national headquarters, listed my qualifications and the jobs I've had here . . . At the moment, I am the manager of the West Atlantic Trust Bank branch on 16th Street. My sister, they pay me more than twice the salary of the Director of the Guinea Coast Commercial Bank. But I was still prepared to sacrifice and go home to help build the economy. I never heard from them. Not a word . . .'

He paused, expecting applause which he got from some of them in the form of nodding heads accompanied by cries of 'Yes, yes . . .' 'He is right.' 'Me too.' 'Me too.'

'. . . So you see, Sissie, I am making good money here and living as well as any Black man can live in these parts. Yet I decided I'll give it all up and just take one third of my present gross. Since it is clear that our country cannot afford my services. After all that, what else can I do? What else would you like me to do?' Pause.

I was going to tell him to go to hell, naturally . . .

My Dear, you teased me once that with a mouth like mine, I don't need a foul temper. Seriously, that's exactly what I have. Both. And a most dangerous combination to live with, in any place at any time . . .

Since you were there at the meeting, I don't have to re-mind you of all the details but they stand so clearly in my mind . . . Before I could scream at the last speaker, the situa-tion was saved for me because all at once, everyone was talking, wanting to give me his side of the story. I thought then that I had better relax and enjoy myself . . . It must be fun being a Catholic priest. Listening to confessions. You know people never really tell you the truth. And you don't really care, since you are not God anyway. Besides what's the point in listening to truth since you suspect that in the long run, it has less colour then the imaginary sins folks would dream up and tell you about?

. . . By speaking up, I had given them the chance they had been dying for, to talk to themselves.

For most, it was the mother thing. Everybody claimed

that he wanted to make sure he did 'something' for 'My Mother.' Send money home to build her a house while they were still abroad or the first thing they did when they got back. 'Because' they would add, 'My Mother has suffered.' Awo, Mama, Ena, Maeto, Nne, Nna, Emama, Iyie . . .

Of course she has suffered, the African mother. Allah, how she has suffered. How much, and for how long? Just look at what's been happening to her children over the last couple of hundred years . . . When she did not have to sell them to local magnates for salt, rampaging strangers kidnapped them to other places where other overlords considered their lives wasted unless at least once before they died, they slept with an African woman. And the titillation was supreme if they could have her brother watching helplessly on – a bonded man. Lord, what we've been through, My Darling . . . Meanwhile, those who grew up around Mother woke up to forced labour and thinly-veiled slavery on colonial plantations . . . Later on, her sons were conscripted into imperial armies and went to die in foreign places, all over again or returned to her, with maimed bodies and minds. And now look at those for whom she's been scrimping, saving and mortgaging her dignity in order to send to school nearby, or abroad. Look at them returning with grandchildren whom she can't communicate with, because they speak only English, French, Portuguese or even German, and she doesn't? Oh yes, she has suffered. So that this low-cost shack distempered in pastel shades they promise her is at least something she knows. But My Dear, don't be angry with me again if you can help it. But isn't there a danger that we might think we are solving a very old corporate problem by applying individual and piece-meal measures? So all of us who have been overseas build houses for our mothers. Then what next?

They talked that evening. My brothers talked. You probably were the only one who never said anything to me then. In fact, through it all, you never said a word. You just stood at that one spot a little near the crowd, watching me, looking very amused and very very handsome. Your beard was shining black black in the light and I wanted so badly to come and touch it. A mere fantasy, since I was caught in the middle of a complete circle . . . In any case, I don't have that kind of courage . . . not when we had not said a word to each other before. After a time I noticed you were not standing there any more and I felt so lonely fearing you had left .

But whether you were there or not, My Love, some of the excuses they gave were so funny. One young man with a little-boy-lost look said that because he is Akan and comes from a matrilineal family, he has more relatives to look after. While his Ewe, Mandingo and other friends with patrilineal backgrounds have it easier! In fact, even his own friends booed at him. Because as someone indignantly reminded him relatives are relatives. Some have them matrilineal and others have them patrilineal. But we all have our share of them. Such sweet anthropology!

Then I met another one of them the other day, when I went to the embassy to renew my passport. And between the two of us, he said that he can't go home yet because he has to take care of an urgent personal problem. He is approaching thirty but he still can't grow a beard. A family trait. He feels such shame. So he has decided to have a hair graft on his chin. It is a very expensive operation, he declared. He is therefore staying to work for a little more money to get it done. Then he would have to wait a year or so while the scars from the surgery healed and he also learnt to feel at ease with his new and permanent beard . . .

Everything was not relaxed that evening. No. Some reactions frightened me. So that I almost regretted that I had spoken. For when a problem is like a big pit, then it must be opened up with a mouth that must surely be more experienced than mine, no? I was sorry for myself. You realised it, didn't you? For surely, that must have been why you had that look on your face . . . Maybe I was even sorrier for them. Since the way they reacted to my brief statement absolved me of all blame. I was only a prancing child who had unwittingly stepped on their sores. Each was nursing his wound. But a wound there was. Open. Bleeding.

'Young Lady, take me for instance . . .' The

speaker was a fairly short gentleman with a 'face you can't abuse into.' He looked much older than anyone else around. He it was who shamed me totally. For all of a sudden I was thinking that it was not really my business what someone like him did with his life. Even though he looked more out of place there than the rest, viewed against a land where Black men are forever regarded as children . . . I didn't know where to put my eyes while that man spoke.

'. . . I have bought houses here. Houses. When my cousin came here on a charter flight last summer, he could not believe it when I told him that I owned my home and more besides. Yes, here. I rent them out to home boys at moderate rates. I am not like those who don't know a countryman from a stranger and cruelly exploit their own people. In fact, ask them, they shall bear witness . . .'

'He is good.' 'Uncle is good,' said some voices.

'The fact that I have lived overseas for all these years does not mean that I have lost my sense of African hospitality . . .' They took it up for him from that point.

'Yes, Sissie, he throws parties for us most holidays, our national holidays.'

'Most of the wedding receptions are given in his house,' someone else shouted from the back. It had developed into a well-planned drama.

'He is the chairman of our Benevolent Society.'

'When any of us dies, he sees to it that the body gets home in good shape.'

'Or they get fitting burials with proper wake-keeping and memorial services . . . None of their plastic funerals for us!'

'You have to admit, Lady, that there has to be someone around these parts to do what Uncle is doing for us . . .'

'Yes, yes.' It was all I could do to keep from laughing into their faces. They cured me of my doubts. For, that last demonstration was too much like politics at home. You know . . . the local politician and his supporters.

'Besides, Uncle worked hard to send himself here and never had a scholarship. Why should he feel obliged to go home?' said somebody.

'Okay, so how about those other thousands all over the western world who were brought here and maintained throughout by government scholarships, and who have refused, consistently, to go back home after graduation?' I knew I was getting irritated. Just then, I heard a new voice, confident, angry.

'Listen, Sister. You cannot make these blanket statements. We came here on government scholarships. So what? Whose scholarships were we to come on? Besides, look at someone like me. Haven't I paid my debt through the distinctions I've been winning?'

I must say: I did look at him. Literally too. Indeed, I did not remove my eyes from his face all the time he talked. You remember him, don't you? I didn't know when you returned to your corner. However, when I saw you there again, I was happy. You later told me that that young doctor was indeed brilliant. That he had not grown snobbish in spite of his achievements and the very fact of his presence at the meeting was a proof of his concern. You also made me understand that normally, he didn't say much and therefore my statement must have hurt him indeed. Dear Heart, you are in the profession and would know whether he is good or not. And this is where what someone has described as my lack of feminine instincts comes in. I probably should have guessed, after we really became good friends, that also precisely because you are in the same field, you might take whatever criticisms I made of the man to be my criticisms of you. Puei, it's all too much. Where would I get this wisdom from? So I argued and quarrelled with you over and over again until you got fed up? Oh no, he was definitely not the whole issue. On the other hand, now I have to admit that he became the symbol of everything that I thought was distasteful about all the folks who have decided to stay overseas permanently. No, none of you admit it as openly as he does: but then, he has the confidence of the long distance runner. Oh My Dear, and all the time you identified with him. Now, what seems like a real miracle is that in spite of everything, you had not walked out on me earlier. My Darling, God bless you for that and many other things. It was so beautiful while it lasted. But it is plain it could not have gone on forever. Love came to us and right from the beginning, it had a case to answer. I should have been a different me. Then I could have pretended that the differences were not so terrible.

Don't say 'pretend.' All of life is a game. Learn to play your part, that's all. Says the voice of forever-wisdom. Hm . . . hm. Hm . . . hm. Hm . . . hm. A few refuse to play. They pay the price, for sure. A few women, a few men too. In my own way, I tried. Maybe that was nothing compared to the extent the smart ones would go. But that's me. So do not judge me too harshly. It is a wild heart but not a mean one. Yet, so is yours . . . And that is enough reason for two people to love one another; yes?

My Darling, I could not 'pretend' to like your brilliant colleague. On that I plead guilty. Why, the man really went on as if I had challenged him to an achievement duel. All in order to explain why he wants to live in Europe and America? For what seemed like half the night, his voice came, steady.

'Listen, listen, listen. I have made our people proud. I have already got to the top of my profession. Gaining recognition as one of the world's ten experts on gastric disorders . . . And anyway, all this preaching at us to come home . . . What is there? Apart from stupid and corrupt civilian regimes, coups, and even more stupid and corrupt military regimes? . . . And then there are one's medical colleagues, who for a long time were the only ones around. Now they have become so mediocre that the only pleasure they seem to get out of life is frustrating younger people. Every time I'm home,' he said, 'I visit some hospitals. It's the same story from the north to the south. They won't do the work and they won't have anyone else do it . . . Indeed, one learns that these days, they don't bother to answer letters from applicants . . . I have never tried to apply. But I know plenty who have. There were two guys who left from this area, concerned types, with some radical political ideas . . . with lots of naïve enthusiasm, your sort! They just packed up one day and went back home. You'll split yoursides, Sister, listening to their stories . . .'

There were cries of 'Oh yes,' 'Oh yes,' from the others. I believe they even murmured out some names.

'Stories about letters calling them to interviews for which none of the panel turned up; of young doctors eventually getting appointed, indeed starting to receive salaries while they are kept out of the hospitals for months and months on the pretext that their bungalows are not ready . . . My Sister, you don't want me to go home only to be frustrated, do you? How could someone like me go back? I can't even see how . . . Now I only do research. No joke. They'll tell you I am becoming the last word in Medical Science as far as the human abdomen is concerned. No conference on the subject is any good if I am not invited. I do the Intestinal-By-Pass as a hobby. Listen, I know that lots of times white people come to me just to verify for themselves that I am indeed an African . . . My fame has spread to Russia and China. Now that's something, no? . . . Sister, there are no facilities at home to provide someone like me with the congenial atmosphere in which to work. And that's a fact! Where are the funds? You may not be aware of it but to equip a first class research set-up for me would swallow the annual budget of the Ministry of Health . . . No, let me stay here a while . . .'

I couldn't say anything to that. What could I say? So much of it was true . . . I was like a stone staring into his animated face.

'. . . We will come home of course. One of these days. I have been going home fairly regularly in the last couple of years anyway. Every year, in fact, to see my mother . . . find out my younger brothers and sisters are doing . . . I support everybody: grandparents, aunts, cousins. And incidentally, I can afford to do all that only because I am still here . . . I have helped lots of relatives to come here too . . . But as I was saying, I am home every winter for at least four weeks. It is necessary for one's perspective. So refreshing. Keeps one in touch with reality. And not only that. It is proving very useful . . . You know that area so often discussed, so much speculated on? The marriage of

African traditional medical insights with western clinical expertise? Well, people just talk. But they have not got the slightest idea of what it's all about. It is an explosion . . . But that was just by the way. What I am trying to tell you is that I have come to regard my annual visit home as a very revitalising process. Other than that, Sister, I feel okay here. And after all, wherever one feels at home must be home. This earth belongs to us all. We can perch anywhere.'

'But we are not birds.' Obviously, I had got myself back.

'What's the difference?' he asked calmly.

'The difference is in everything that you have said tonight. Our needs are more complicated than those of birds, aren't they? Surely our bodies demand more than branches, air, and seeds . . .'

I was groping for a way to tell him what was in my mind. Of life being relevantly lived. Of the intangible realities. Such stuff. Yet I didn't want to get caught up in a lot of metaphysical crap. When an atmosphere is as inert as Africa today, the worst thing you can do to anybody is to sell him your dreams. . . . I needn't have worried because the famous doctor was off on his own tangent again.

'. . . You know how here in the western hemisphere, they still want to believe that the only thing Black people can do is to entertain them? Run, jump and sing? Of course, we Africans have never really succumbed to their image of the Nigger . . .

'. . . But you can see how by remaining here someone like me serves a very useful purpose in educating them to recognise our worth . . .?'

'Educating whom to recognise our worth, My Brother?' I asked.

'The people here,' he said.

'Where?'

'Here, in the West.'

'You mean white people?'

'Well . . . yes . . .'

'But they have always known how much we are worth. They have always known that, My Brother, and a whole lot more. They may not consider it necessary to openly admit it . . . that's another matter. They probably know it is strategically unwise to. You see . . . My Brother, if we are not careful, we would burn out our brawn and brains trying to prove what you describe as "our worth" and we won't get a flicker of recognition from those cold blue eyes. And anyway, who are they? . . . So please come home, My Brother. Come to our people. They are the only ones who need to know how much we are worth. The rewards would not be much. Hardly anything. For every successful surgery, they will hail you as a miracle worker. Because their faith will not be in the knives you wield but in your hands; in your human touch . . . Once in a year; some man of means will come to give you thanks, with a sheep. Or a goat. Sometimes they may even make a subtle hint that you marry their beautiful daughter . . ..

'But most of the time, it will be humble expressions of humbler means. A hen. A cockerel. An old woman would carry you eggs laid by home-reared chicken. A widow might bring you her last tuber of yam . . . No, these days uncertainties of reception is stopping even such gestures. So most of the time, it will be plain old verbal "thank-you" very timidly said, and in silence, a blessing of the womb that bore you . . .'

My Darling, I hadn't been aware that I was making a speech. When I paused, the silence made itself heard. I looked up and there were so many eyes. Then I realised that the doctor was holding the hands of a white woman . . . Allah, I meant to ask you later about her. Who was she? His wife or just a girlfriend?

. . . Anyhow, something was threatening to collapse in me then . . . So this is it? We are only back to square one, yes? The superior monkey has got his private white audience for whom he performs his superior tricks. Proving our worth, eh? I was close to tears . . . Just then you came. Walked straight to me and took my hands. Oh My Dear, My Precious, My Own Something, how shall I ever thank you for that moment? We couldn't have done better if we had timed it. You remember leading me out of the hall with the voices close behind us, then a broad murmur and finally fading away, while outside in the cold night, the shining snow looked so hard I thought it was always there, then you driving and driving and driving, then out of the car, and you pulling my coat closer around me and saying you didn't think it was heavy enough, then up some elevator, you opening a door, taking my coat, sitting me down in a chair, pouring me some liquor, you didn't even ask me whether I drank or not and what, and I was grateful, and you pouring yourself a drink too, and sitting yourself down in a chair, right opposite me and with the smile around your eyes, you saying, 'I know everyone calls you Sissie, but what is your name?'

The aeroplane nosed its way through the air, cutting up the clouds. With nearly three hundred people on board, it was plainly too big to almost obscene proportions when considered as an air vehicle. Yet there were already noises around of new ones getting built which might be twice the size of the one in which Sissie was travelling back. And faster.

Inside the plane, there were quite a few of the pacifiers for the jagged nerves that most air travellers suffer from, no matter how often they fly or how long. There was music on about eight channels. And just fading off the screen was a bleary film of the American Wild West, dating from the early days of motion pictures. The service crew, apart from passing around sweets, soft drinks and liquor, were also doing some brisk business selling cigarettes, perfume and other familiar duty-free rubbish. And meanwhile, people of different shades and motivations were also actively passing all kinds of classified information around, with each pair involved in a transaction thinking they were the cleverest undercover agents on board. Altogether, the atmosphere was that of another human market-place.

Sissie is the kind of passenger over whose head such activities normally go unnoticed. Flying makes her supremely nervous and she often reads endlessly. On this particular flight, she had been doing something else. Writing the letter.

'Ladies and gentlemen . . .' The voice announced the altitude they were flying at, the temperature outside, the

speed of the wind and added that they would be leaving the
Atlantic in a minute and in fact, if they looked down, they
would see the continent of Africa . . .

Sissie woke up. She had been completely absorbed in what
she was doing . . . Sure enough, there was Africa, huge and
from this coastline, certainly warm and green. In fact, she
responded less to the voice from the pilot's cabin than the
heat which suddenly hit the plane and invaded its chilly
interiors.

When she realised that she had been writing all the time
they had been in the air, she was amazed. The letter was
deservedly long. Over the next couple of stops, she read and
reread it. Somehow, the more she read it, the more relieved
she felt. That she had actually written it. Yet she felt somewhat uneasy too. It was definitely too long and anyway,
what did she hope to achieve by sending it to him? She had
thought of asking the stewardesses for some of their envelopes
so that she would divide the letter into about three packages
and drop them into the nearest airport mailbox. And now
she was not sure she wanted to do that, not yet . . . She
had once heard that this type of post mortem correspondence
doesn't do much good. In fact, if you asked the know-
ledgeable ones, they would tell you it is a bad policy. But
then, so great had been her need to communicate. What
was she to do? . . .

She sat quietly in her seat and stared at the land unfolding
before her. Dry land, trees, a swamp, more dry land, green,
green, lots of green. She had to check herself from laughing
aloud. Suddenly, she knew what she was not going to do.
She was never going to post the letter. Once written, it was
written. She had taken some of the pain away and she was
glad. There was no need to mail it. It was not necessary.
She was going to let things lie where they had fallen. Besides,
she was back in Africa. And that felt like fresh honey on the
tongue: a mixture of complete sweetness and smoky rough-
age. Below was home with its unavoidable warmth and even
after these thousands of years, its uncertainties.

'Oh, Africa. Crazy old continent . . .'

Sissie wondered whether she had spoken aloud to herself.

The occupant of the next seat probably thought she was crazy. Then she decided she didn't care anyway.

Also in Longman African Writers

The Dilemma of a Ghost and Anowa

Ama Ata Aidoo

These two witty and perceptive social dramas are sympathetic and honest explorations of the conflicts between the individualism of westernised culture and the social traditions of Africa. Both plays have been performed to audiences throughout the world and reinforce Ama Ata Aidoo's position as one of the leading creative voices in Africa today.

Dilemma of a Ghost

When Ato returns to Ghana from his studies in North America he brings with him a sophisticated black American wife. But their hopes of a happy marriage and of combining the 'sweetest and loveliest things in Africa and America' are soon shown to have been built on an unstable foundation.

Anowa

Based on an old Ghanaian legend, *Anowa* is the story of a young woman who decides, against her parents' wishes, to marry the man she loves. After many trials and tribulations the couple amass a fortune — but Anowa realises that something, somewhere is wrong.

Ama Ata Aidoo has a gift for the sparse economical language of sadness and despair and for the gaiety, rollicking boisterousness and acid wit of comedy, satire, irony and parady:
African Literature Today

ISBN 0 582 00244 3

No Sweetness Here

Ama Ata Aidoo

"There is no use in screaming about how independent you are by driving away the colonialists if you do not make independence meaningful."

Ama Ata Aidoo

In these stories, which range from the politics of wigs to the fragile joy of maternity, Ama Ata Aidoo, one of Africa's leading woman writers, speaks with forthright honesty about life in post-colonial Africa. She does not dodge awkward issues but nor does she give in to feelings of hopelessness. Instead, she invites the reader to confront life as it is and to rise to the challenge of injustice and ignorance.

"Some stories are about village people and life; others about conflict and confusions for town's people. They are beautifully written"

The English Magazine

'a subtle critism that cuts as sharply as a razor. There is not a single dull story in the eleven.'

Daily Nation

ISBN 0 582 00393 8

Other Titles available

Longman African Writers

Other Titles Available

Longman Caribbean Writers

All these titles are available from your local bookseller. For further information on these titles, and study guides available contact your local Longman agent or Addison Wesley Longman Limited, Edinburgh Gate, Harlow, Essex, CM20 2JE, England.